Bolan pulled the pin
and hurled the grenade

He raced back into the woods and crouched behind the largest tree he could find. The big trunk suddenly snapped hard into Bolan's back, sending him sprawling to the ground. The instant vacuum created by the explosion sucked the air from his lungs, making him gasp and choke for breath.

As the warrior's lungs filled again, they drew in more fumes than air and he coughed painfully. Bolan tried to roll under the tangle of branches, but he was pinned. He struggled and managed to lift his head enough to examine the compound. The devastation was horrendous.

Vittorio Muro had escaped, taking Emily Grant with him. But the leader of the Union Corse had just made a formidable enemy.

Summoning all his strength, Bolan heaved a twisted branch aside, vowing with grim resolve to rescue the Fox Den agent. And if Muro got in the way...so much the better.

MACK BOLAN ®

The Executioner

#60 Sold for Slaughter
#61 Tiger War
#62 Day of Mourning
#63 The New War Book
#64 Dead Man Running
#65 Cambodia Clash
#66 Orbiting Omega
#67 Beirut Payback
#68 Prairie Fire
#69 Skysweeper
#70 Ice Cold Kill
#71 Blood Dues
#72 Hellbinder
#73 Appointment in Kabul
#74 Savannah Swingsaw
#75 The Bone Yard
#76 Teheran Wipeout
#77 Hollywood Hell
#78 Death Games
#79 Council of Kings
#80 Running Hot
#81 Shock Waves
#82 Hammerhead Reef
#83 Missouri Deathwatch
#84 Fastburn
#85 Sunscream
#86 Hell's Gate
#87 Hellfire Crusade
#88 Baltimore Trackdown
#89 Defenders and Believers
#90 Blood Heat Zero
#91 The Trial
#92 Moscow Massacre
#93 The Fire Eaters
#94 Save the Children
#95 Blood and Thunder
#96 Death Has a Name
#97 Meltdown
#98 Black Dice
#99 Code of Dishonor
#100 Blood Testament
#101 Eternal Triangle

#102 Split Image
#103 Assault on Rome
#104 Devil's Horn
#105 Countdown to Chaos
#106 Run to Ground
#107 American Nightmare
#108 Time to Kill
#109 Hong Kong Hit List
#110 Trojan Horse
#111 The Fiery Cross
#112 Blood of the Lion
#113 Vietnam Fallout
#114 Cold Judgment
#115 Circle of Steel
#116 The Killing Urge
#117 Vendetta in Venice
#118 Warrior's Revenge
#119 Line of Fire
#120 Border Sweep
#121 Twisted Path
#122 Desert Strike
#123 War Born
#124 Night Kill
#125 Dead Man's Tale
#126 Death Wind
#127 Kill Zone

Stony Man Doctrine
Terminal Velocity
Resurrection Day
Dirty War
Flight 741
Dead Easy
Sudden Death
Rogue Force
Tropic Heat
Fire in the Sky
Anvil of Hell
Flash Point
Flesh and Blood
Moving Target
Tightrope

DON PENDLETON's EXECUTIONER

MACK BOLAN®

Kill Zone

A GOLD EAGLE BOOK FROM

WORLDWIDE®

TORONTO • NEW YORK • LONDON • PARIS
AMSTERDAM • STOCKHOLM • HAMBURG
ATHENS • MILAN • TOKYO • SYDNEY

First edition July 1989

ISBN 0-373-61127-7

Special thanks and acknowledgment to
Carl Furst for his contribution to this work.

It is not granted to know which man took up arms
with more right on his side. Each pleads his cause
before a great judge: The winning cause pleased the
gods, but the losing one pleased Cato.

—Lucan A.D. 39–65
Bellum Civile, I.126

I am not their judge, I am their judgment. I am their
executioner.

—Mack Bolan

Dedicated to the
international policing agencies
who fight an endless war
against the proliferation
of illegal drugs.

1

Mack Bolan sat in the crowded taverna in Athens, his back to the wall, waiting for the two agents he'd been urged to meet to make their appearance.

Bob Millard, of Fox Den, arrived first, alone, and established his identity to Bolan's satisfaction. He'd telephoned the night before, saying Hal Brognola, Director of the Sensitive Operations Group, United States Department of Justice, had told him how to make the contact.

Bolan had checked with Brognola before he agreed to the meet. He had access to the Fed through a special communications link operated jointly by the National Security Agency and the Sensitive Operations Group. Brognola could contact him, too, by leaving certain codes in places where Bolan would check.

"Yeah, Striker," the big Fed had said. "I suggested to Millard that he get in touch with you. Bob's bona fide. He's a Fox Den agent. You know much about that agency?"

"I've heard of it," Bolan replied. He'd been hearing about it for almost a year, in fact—the new, highly specialized, supersecret agency created to fight the powerful dealers who were flooding city streets in every country with more heroin and cocaine than was imaginable. He'd run into its agents here and there, and was grateful for an effective ally. "Can I trust Millard?"

"Yeah, and he's good, Striker. He's survived some pretty rough fights—Europe, the Middle East, South America. He works very differently than you. He doesn't take the risks you take nor get fast results. He's an educated man, a lifelong government man who studies, ponders, considers, reconsiders. He'd drive you nuts, the way he works. But he's done some damned good work."

"You aren't trying to give me a partner, are you, Hal?"

"No way, Striker. I gave up on that a long time ago. I'd appreciate it, though, if you'd see the guy. He's onto something that's worth looking into. Let me give you a little more on the guy. He's got a female partner with him who's tougher than he is and just as effective. Pretty, too. It'd be easy for a man to fall for her. Hard."

"Okay, Hal. Let me make my own judgment on that. Just feed me the intel."

ANYONE LOOKING at Robert Millard might have guessed the man was a failed Harvard lawyer, someone who hadn't made partner in one of the big-firm pissing contests, or maybe a senior clerk in a firm of London solicitors.

In truth, he wasn't a lawyer and never had been. As Hal Brognola had described him, Millard was a lifelong servant of his government, a foreign-service officer out of Georgetown University at first, then a realistic player of the intelligence game, finally an operative for Fox Den, where he devoted his not-inconsiderable talents to just the kind of problem he wanted to discuss with Bolan.

"I've got a partner with me," Millard said. "Emily Grant. She'll be with us in a few minutes. Let me tell you a little bit about her before she comes."

"Brognola filled me in."

"Let me tell you a little more." Millard insisted. "You might be surprised by Emily. She's no shrinking violet. She holds a brown belt in judo, and when she can give the time to the training, she'll undoubtedly get the black belt. If she decides she wants it, she'll get it. I can tell you that for sure. Besides that, she's an expert with small arms and the knife."

"No shrinking violet," Bolan said dryly.

"She's fluent in French, German, Spanish, Italian and Arabic, and can understand and make herself understood in Russian, Chinese and Japanese. That's why she's assigned to this case."

"Experience?" Bolan asked.

"She came to Fox Den from the Defense Intelligence Agency. I don't know what she did for them. Nobody tells you what happens there, unless you have a real need to know. With Fox Den... Well, it's the same. But I can tell you Emily's got experience. And guts. If anything, she's got too much in the way of guts."

"Reckless?"

Millard frowned then shook his head. "She wouldn't be alive if she was reckless, any more than you would. She's smart."

"You're impressed," Bolan observed. "Hal told me she made a vivid impression."

"She's a formidable young woman. Our code name for her is Vixen—the bitch fox. She doesn't like that much."

Just as their waiter placed a bottle of wine on the table—not the bitter Greek retsina of the house, but a tourist wine—Emily Grant arrived. She was a blond, her complexion was fair and her cheeks were pink, as if constantly flushed. Her hair was cut close to her head. She wasn't tall. Though slender, even slight, the muscles in her arms and legs were taut cords. Her breasts were fascinatingly prominent.

"Well," she said to Millard, "how much have you told him?"

"Only what a lovely girl you are, Emily," Millard replied. "We didn't start without you."

The meeting then got under way with a recruiting spiel.

"I assume you checked with Brognola after you got my call, Mr. Bolan. I don't know how much he told you, so let us tell you that we need you. We know something about your special combination of talent and experience, and we don't have anyone else available who does what you do."

"Which isn't an easy admission for us, frankly," Emily put in. "We like to think we're getting pretty good and don't have to call in specialists. But—"

"But the job we have in mind needs your skills and knowledge," Millard interrupted. "I think you'll like the way we operate. We do what we have to do, we don't ask many questions and we answer hardly any."

"You will sooner or later," Bolan said. "A government agency always has to, sometime. You know, accountability in a democracy. That's one reason I make a point of working independently."

Millard didn't argue the point. "We know you won't come to work for us. What we'd like, however, is some cooperation on this particular job. Let me tell you about it, anyway."

"I'm listening."

"It's a tough one," he began. "Uh, first names, okay? You can call us Bob and Emily. So, we think we know what's going on, but—"

"It's pretty clear, I think," Emily interrupted. "Anyway, it's becoming clear."

"Big-time dealers started to bite the dust. At first we thought maybe *you* were killing them," Millard said. "In New York, there was Perugio and Mendoza . . . We thought—"

"I never thought it was Bolan," Emily Grant denied. "Torturing men to death—even big-time drug merchants—isn't his style."

"That's true," Millard agreed. "They were tortured to death."

"As was Dubois in Marseilles," Emily said. "Piombo in Italy—"

"Others," Millard added. "None in the Far East, though. Just the Europeans and Americans. It was easy to think someone was doing us a favor, but believe me, they weren't. The stuff dried up for a short time, then we began to see a flood of it. Heroin. Cocaine. Better quality, too, I'm sorry to say. More refined. More powerful."

"In other words, a new crowd of suppliers moved in," Bolan concluded.

Millard nodded. "Only at the top level. It's the same old gang of pushers at street level, and the same old gang between them and the big suppliers. It's only the top suppliers who've changed, the guys who move it across the borders. The stuff is better, and the price is higher."

"The old crowd was capable of fighting back," Bolan said. "They got where they were because they were willing to kill anyone who got in their way."

"They were never as vicious as this," Millard told him. "Listen, there've been other things—planes blown up, boats sunk. The old crowd killed. I mean, in the past we could identify a couple of hundred deaths a year, the result of their power struggles, their enforcement. But the new crowd, Mack, we've identified two hundred killed in the past *month*. Somebody's moving in on the trade with a ruthlessness nobody ever dreamed of before."

"Go on," Bolan prompted.

"The stuff is coming in from the Middle East. It's like the growers themselves have decided to eliminate the middlemen."

"Iran is a bigger source than ever," Emily continued. "Except for the Golden Triangle in Southeast

Asia, northern Iran and eastern Turkey are the biggest sources."

"A few years ago, refugees from the ayatollahs funded themselves by carrying out morphine base. This is different," Millard added.

"Even so," Bolan said, "where are their enforcers? Who's organizing? A gang of poppy farmers, no matter how well they've organized themselves, isn't murdering big operators like Perugio and Mendoza in New York. To go to war against hard-case types like those requires tough men and a lot of them. Who's supplying the organizational talent?"

"That we haven't figured out," Emily admitted.

"Iranians," Bolan said, "Turks, Iraqis, Afghans. Admirable people in many ways, and certainly tough fighters, but they don't know Queens from Staten Island, Malibu from Disneyland. There has to be somebody else involved."

"We've got a bit of information," Millard said. "From sources we regard as reliable, we believe a major shipment of morphine base will be transferred from land transport to sea transport on Friday night, at a point on the Syrian coast just north of Al-Ladhiqiyah. If you were there—"

"Let me be specific," Emily Grant interrupted grimly. "If you are there, you can interrupt the transfer of the shipment. That shipment alone is enough to foster a heroin epidemic in the United States, if it gets there. If after that you can discover who's doing what and how, that will be a bonus."

"We have reason to believe," Millard added, "that the shipment is to be moved from land transport to a flag-carrying warship of Colonel Khaddafi. It will fly the Libyan flag. So it is officially a ship of the Libyan navy. Do you understand?"

"Yes. Half the nations that might want to stop the shipment are afraid to touch that Libyan boat because they're afraid of an international incident," Bolan said.

"Afraid he'll cut off their oil," Emily added. "When the choice is to ignore a major shipment of morphine base—most of which will arrive, ultimately, in the States—or to risk a hundred thousand cold apartments in Paris next winter, or a million cars not running for want of gasoline, the French government will let the morphine base go through. So will others."

"It's worse than that," Millard said. "The government of the United States isn't willing, at present, to attack a flag-carrying warship of an Arab country on the high seas. We have every reason to believe this Libyan patrol boat is a constant carrier of morphine base—plus plastique for terrorists and God knows what else—all through the Mediterranean. The government of the United States isn't yet willing to touch it. But if you were to—"

"Sink the son of a bitch," Emily said.

"No!" Millard exclaimed. "We can't. We don't dare. There are larger issues involved."

Emily Grant smiled. "Not with American weapons. Not as an identified American agent." Her smile broadened. "Of course, if you found some way to do it

so that the identification couldn't be established...
Discretion forbids my saying more."

"Discretion would tell me not to get myself involved. Are you sure of your information?"

Millard smiled. "If you know anything about Fox
Den, you know our information is accurate. Getting
information is our specialty. Sometimes we turn to
others to make the best use of it, but—"

"Okay," Bolan said. "There's a lot at stake in this
one. I'll work with you this time. Next time..." He
shrugged.

"Good enough," Millard replied. "I won't even
shake hands with you on it. Not exactly appropriate, is
it?"

BOLAN REMAINED in the café with Emily Grant for an
hour after Millard left. He saw fading bruises and faint
scars on her wrists. Sometime in the not-too-distant
past, Emily had been handcuffed—very tightly and
probably for a long time, and she had struggled against
the manacles and injured her wrists. He recognized
wisdom in her eyes. Emily was no girl. She was a young
woman who had seen much of the world, and most
likely, some of the worst.

"You like the real Greek wine?" she asked.

He nodded. "How'd you get the cuffs off, Emily?"

"Took the key out of a dead man's pocket," she replied.

"I shouldn't have asked. Sure, I like Greek wine.
Bitter stuff, but good. I suppose you do mean the retsina?"

"That's what I mean," she said, summoning the waiter.

"Figures. How did you get into this business?"

"It was just something that I had to do," she stated simply.

Bolan nodded and looked around the café, alert and cautious as always, aware that the people whose purposes they were out to frustrate could strike coldly at any time, any place, if they recognized a threat to whatever it was they were planning.

"It was a would-be hero who got me into handcuffs, in a cellar room. In an old coal bin, as a matter of fact, in Philadelphia." She hesitated for a moment, then shook off whatever thought had stopped her. "White slavers. They thought they had a real prize in me, if you know what I mean. Until— Well, even in the service of humanity there's just so much you can take. I defended myself, as we might way. He yelled for his buddies, and the next thing I know, I'm on my belly on a wet brick floor, hands behind my back."

"And you killed a guy and got the key?"

She nodded. "It's something of a trick when your hands are cuffed behind your back, but it can be done. I understand you let a woman trick you once," she said, then abruptly changed the subject and the mood of the conversation.

The corners of his mouth had flickered in and out of a quick grin. "Once? I've been fooled by a pretty face more than once."

2

Mack Bolan crouched in the dry grass at the edge of a beach a few miles north of Al-Ladhiqiyah, watching the vehicle approach in darkness that was relieved only by the faintly phosphorescent glow of the breakers. The night smelled of sea death—the distinctive heavy odor of the saltwater creatures who wash ashore and die on the sand. Four and five-foot breakers crashed on the wet sand and rushed up the beach, almost reaching Bolan's position.

The engine and transmission groaned as the vehicle wallowed in the beach sand. He could see it distinctly now, outlined against the faint luminescence of the rolling, crashing water. Though the driver kept the headlights dark—perhaps under the impression his noisy vehicle wouldn't be noticed if his headlights weren't on—Bolan recognized the silhouette as that of a Dodge Power Wagon, the rugged all-terrain vehicle Americans had shipped to the Middle Eastern oil fields by the thousands. He saw two little points of orange light that could only be cigarettes or cigars. He judged that four men were in the ATV.

He thought he saw the silhouette of a light machine gun, somehow mounted on a vehicle not meant to carry one. Whether he was right about that or not, he was certain these four men would be heavily armed. The business they were in, they would have to be.

Bolan checked his own weapons. The .44 Desert Eagle was sheathed in leather against his right thigh. For situations that required something quieter, the warrior carried a specially modified 9 mm Beretta in a shoulder holster. The 93-R was equipped with a sound suppressor that would reduce its authoritative crack to a throaty burp. Various pouches on his belt contained extra clips of ammunition for each pistol, knives and other weapons the Executioner would need for this hit.

The driver of the Dodge wasn't smart. He kept to the dry sand, well back from the surf, and away from the hard wet sand. Consequently his wheels churned and his engine protested. Despite the handicap, the vehicle came on, finally stopping only twenty yards from where Bolan lay concealed.

The warrior glanced around. The hardmen in the vehicle seemed to be working with the same landmark as his own—a fragment of ruined ancient temple on a hill behind the beach about a quarter mile away. Twice since he'd been there, he'd seen a green light flash between the two truncated columns of that jagged ruin. Someone was signaling to a ship at sea. And now, with the vehicle there on the beach, the green light flashed again. The four men—and there were definitely four; he could count them now—weren't the only ones involved on the land side of this operation.

He had to work quietly. The men in the Power Wagon were enough to deal with; he didn't want their confederates rushing down. What was more important, he didn't want whoever was flashing the green light to flash a signal that would warn off the ship. Bolan wanted to see that ship.

He moved to a position more advantageous for watching the newcomers. The four men began to unload something big and heavy from the vehicle, shouting at one another in voices obviously angry and anxious.

The warrior couldn't make out what they were saying. One of them loudly played leader and wore traditional Arab garb—a robe and burnoose. Two of his companions moved awkwardly because they were unwilling to unshoulder their automatic weapons. The fourth—if Bolan judged right—was more the leader than the Arab who barked orders: a quiet, efficient man who knew what he was doing and tolerated the ostensible leadership of the robed man.

The men wrestled their heavy burden onto the sand—an inflated boat, which was twin-hulled and equipped with an outboard motor. Three of the Arabs began to drag it toward the water, grunting and heaving, while the fourth—the robed leader—remained with the Dodge and occupied himself with the rest of the load.

What remained in the back of the vehicle was morphine base—bales of it, an epidemic of addiction bundled into neat packages and carried in this small vehicle to the beach where it would be transferred to a ship lying out there somewhere and receiving light signals from the temple behind the beach.

What did they have there? Two hundred kilos? Three hundred? Three hundred kilograms—almost seven hundred pounds—of agony and death. Worth millions of dollars on the streets of European and American cities.

The chief—the man who snapped out orders—idled at the rear of the vehicle, slapping the bundles, much like a man slapping a nubile girl across the rump. If his thoughts were of his profits, they were his last thoughts. He was completely unaware of Bolan's approach. A garrote dropped over the man's head, slipped silently past his eyes and was jerked abruptly and decisively into his throat. By the time comprehension worked its way to his consciousness, the guy was dead.

Bolan knelt over his fallen adversary. The guy wasn't Arab from what he could see of him in the dim light, just some Mediterranean hardcase who had chosen to affect Arab dress.

The Executioner moved to the vehicle and cut open one of the bales. The morphine base was brownish-white powder that could have been almost anything. But the smell was distinctive.

One of the hardmen scrambled back toward the vehicle through the loose sand. He wore dungarees and carried an automatic weapon slung over his shoulder. As he approached he brought it around and rested it in his hands. He was wary. Men who had lived through the chaotic horrors of the Middle East tended to be cautious—and quick to kill.

The man spotted the body lying at the rear of the Dodge. The muzzle of the weapon jerked up instantly, pointing squarely at Bolan as if the man had instinctively known where the warrior was. But the man was merely searching the darkness and hadn't seen the black-clad figure with the combat cosmetics smeared on his face. After a brief moment the hardman swung the muzzle away from the vehicle. He probed the darkness in all directions, searching for the man who had killed his commander.

Bolan knew that Dungarees would cry for help at any moment. He leaped from the vehicle and drove his fist into the man's throat, instantly cutting off any possibility of his shouting out. The man was solid and wiry, and though he was choking and in agony from the blow to his Adam's apple, he retained the presence of mind to drop his rifle—which would only have been an impediment in this kind of hand-to-hand combat—and to rely on his hands. He pounded hard on Bolan's kidneys.

The warrior gritted his teeth against the sharp sting of pain in his back and chopped his enemy on the bridge of the nose. The man went limp, groaning with pain. Bolan slashed the throat again, harder. Dungarees choked and fell to the ground, dead.

Two men left. Two on one. Better odds.

The warrior circled the Power Wagon.

"Ay-yah!" The command came floating up from the beach.

The remaining hardmen were impatient, and impatience bred carelessness.

Another gunner returned to the vehicle, creeping forward cautiously with his weapon out before him, finger on the trigger. The fourth man—the one Bolan had recognized as the true leader—followed close behind.

The Executioner pulled the knife from his belt and flipped it through the air in a motion made skillful by long practice. It whispered through the air and stabbed into the abdomen of the gunman. He dropped to his knees, groaning, and tried to pull the knife out. The guy mightn't die, Bolan supposed, but he was out of commission. The man knelt in the sand, clutching the wound that bled through his fingers.

"You're Bolan, I suppose," the fourth man said coldly. He spoke into the darkness, where he thought the warrior might be; he couldn't see him.

"What makes you think you know who I am?"

"Who else? Our sources warned us that you were supposedly in the area. You are going to kill me now." The man seemed to shrug, though it was difficult for Bolan to see the gesture in the darkness. "So be it. But now we know for certain you are here."

"*You* know it. And if I kill you, you take it to the grave."

"We'll all know it." The man's face was obscure in the darkness, no more than a shadow. The shadow kept moving; the man was searching urgently, still hoping to spot the warrior and get off a shot at him.

"You can't prevent me," the voice from the shadows continued, "from firing the pistol I hold in my hand. And when I do, my friends will be warned. They will flee, or they will come to face you—more powerful than you could have dreamed. It makes no difference. You cannot stop us. We are too much for you. We know who you are and what you have done, but you have never confronted anyone like us before. Enjoy your last triumph, Mack Bolan. It is over.''

The sharp crack of a pistol echoed across the night. The bullet kicked up a puff of sand and whined away harmlessly into the night. Bolan drew the Beretta and dropped the fourth man.

The warrior looked toward the temple. Lights were flashing between the two columns—white lights. He looked out to sea and saw no response.

BOLAN HAD LITTLE TIME. His first instinct was to pour gasoline over the load of morphine and set it afire. But that would eliminate any chance he had of identifying the ship at sea, much less doing anything about it.

He began ripping open the bales with his knife. His priority was to destroy this load. If nothing else was accomplished tonight, that much had to be done.

The Executioner climbed behind the wheel of the Dodge and started the engine. He jammed the transmission into first gear. The vehicle seemed to sense the touch of a driver better attuned to machinery than the crazy who had wrestled it through the sand, and it responded obediently to his hands on the gearshift and wheel. He let out the clutch and the Dodge lurched forward. The vehicle was in the surf up to its windshield before the engine coughed on an ingestion of salt water through its air intake and died with an offended jerk.

In minutes the incoming tide would cover the Dodge, and the millions of dollars' worth of morphine base would float away on a flood of brine.

Now what could he do about the flashing lights, or about the ship lying offshore, waiting for a multimillion-dollar shipment?

Bolan had come prepared. He jogged up the beach toward a cache of weapons he'd left waiting for whatever opportunity might present itself. He gathered them into his arms and trotted back toward the big inflated boat that was now rising and falling in the surf. He heaved his weapons into the boat.

Someone from the temple ruins was heading for the beach. *Two* someones, approaching incautiously with flashlights. Obviously they had no idea that all four of their comrades had been killed. They were merely coming to see what was going on.

Bolan watched as the two bobbing lights came nearer. He could fight them, but he had a better idea. He shoved the inflatable boat into the surf, scrambled aboard and used a paddle to push the boat into the roaring breakers. It slipped from shore into deeper water. He paddled, taking great strong strokes that moved the boat up the face of breakers and let him slide down their backs and on out to sea.

When he was beyond the huge waves he moved over to the outboard motor. It started easily and he headed the boat toward the open sea.

The flashlights reached the beach. No doubt the men had found the bodies of their comrades. Bolan leveled the big .44 in a two-hand grip and emptied the magazine. He didn't hit either man, he supposed, but the authoritative roar of the Desert Eagle, the glaring muzzle-flash and the whining bullets put them to flight. But more importantly, he could see heavy breakers washing over the swamped Dodge, washing the slashed bales of morphine into the churning water. Mission accomplished. First priority.

LAND RECEDED. The inflatable boat was eminently seaworthy, driven with minimal roar by the big outboard mounted between its two pontoons. Bolan turned the prow away from land. Without a compass or anything else for navigation, he simply put his stern to the fading lights of the Syrian shore and the faint tinge of dawn that was beginning to bring gray into the black night.

These were fabled waters, seas sailed by heroes and villains since the dawn of history. Not far west was Cyprus. A few miles south lay tortured Beirut. Some distance north, on the Turkish coast, was Antioch. Saint Paul, on his way to Athens, Rome and martyrdom, had coasted these waters. Wars had been fought over this sea for centuries. The bottom was littered, no doubt, with the skeletons of ships sunk by navies as ancient as the pharaohs, and aircraft by the hundreds shot down in the fight for Cyprus during the Second World War. The rubber boat surged forward, it seemed, among the hovering spirits of tens of centuries.

He wondered what those ancient warriors, or even the recent ones, the heroes of the 1940s, would think of the new war. They had fought every kind of enemy—tyrants, emperors, fanatics. But had any of them fought the vicious oppressors he was fighting now—murderers who poisoned children thousands of miles away without ever seeing them and did it for nothing but profit? However corrupt, even diabolical, the ancient villains were, some of them at least had a cause, something more than just making themselves richer and more powerful. Some of them murdered children. Few of them made it a business.

Behind him a faint rosy pink colored the sky and defined the clouds. Abruptly it was possible to distinguish clouds, ranks of them standing above the blurred line of the Syrian shore: some bottomed with gray, brightening with the still-weak sunlight. Dawn was at least an hour away, but this beautiful time of day was refreshing to him.

Bolan had a decision to make. He could hardly go back the way he'd come, to a beach where, if the men with flashlights didn't lay in wait for him, the Syrian authorities might want an answer as to why four dead bodies lay on the beach.

A landfall of Cyprus was eighty miles away—four hours, maybe five. According to information he'd gathered earlier, if he turned northeast, a landfall outside Antioch was sixty miles. He might have felt safer coasting south to Haifa, where the Israeli authorities would know his name, but that was two hundred miles, and he doubted the Evinrude's tank carried enough fuel to make it. He could, if he stayed at sea all day and overnight, return to Jablah from where he'd started out. But he couldn't return to the beach there in an inflatable boat that hadn't been his when he left his hotel the previous night.

Cyprus was probably his best choice—that and a call to the United States Embassy in Nicosia. He unscrewed the cap of the gas tank on the Evinrude. Enough. He could cover the eighty miles.

Bolan set his course west, without a compass, relying on the rising sun to his stern. He could hardly miss Cyprus. It was a big island.

Suddenly he spotted an attack boat streaking toward him at thirty-five knots, the sleekest craft of its type he'd ever seen, riding high and proud over the six-foot waves.

The warrior knew the type—he'd been briefed. It was a French-built boat of the Combattante II-class—a 234-ton, forty-seven-meter, missile-carrying naval patrol boat. His contact had told him the Combattante was armed with four Exocet missile launchers, plus a variety of guns in calibers ranging from 76 mm to a 40 mm antiaircraft mount. A bubble on its forward mast shielded fire-control radar. The patrol boat carried a crew of between twenty-five and forty men and could range the entire eastern Mediterranean on the fuel it carried for its powerful diesels.

Bolan peered into the morning mist at the ensign flying from the stern. It was the solid green banner of Colonel Khaddafi—the Libyan national flag. The boat was more than seven hundred miles from her home port and arrogantly carried the colonel's ensign into the world's most troubled waters. With the deadly Exocets on board, the colonel could afford to dare it.

The bow wave subsided. The high roar of the engines faded to a gurgling rumble as they were throttled back. A light on the bridge began to blink green, a signal. Maybe the captain had missed the signal from shore and thought he was still making rendezvous with the rubber boat, to take aboard the load of morphine base. Or maybe he'd received another signal, that the morphine had been destroyed, the men who had transported it had been killed and the rubber boat had been stolen.

Either way the Libyan boat meant death to Bolan. As it swung around and reversed its engines to stop alongside him thirty yards away, he pulled the canvas off his weapons. A man at sea in a flimsy rubber boat, he had no choice but to attack this heavily armed naval vessel. He had a moment, no more, to attack before *he* was attacked.

The Libyan patrol boat lay gently wallowing in the sea. Someone on the bridge was speaking rapidly through a bullhorn in an Arabic dialect Bolan couldn't understand. He understood something else, though. A black-clad man at the rail just behind the bridge had leveled a machine gun and was getting ready to open fire.

Bolan's own weapons were antiques. The government of the United States couldn't be involved in any scheme to sink a Libyan warship on the high seas. Nothing that could be identified with the United States could be used. If a bit of shrapnel from one of the sophisticated new American hand-held projectile launchers was found in the body of a Libyan sailor washed ashore... Well, Bolan understood.

He'd gone shopping and found what he was now unwrapping from the stinking old canvas they'd been wrapped in for forty years. The weapons still worked, the dealer had promised; he'd seen one fired only a few months earlier.

Panzerfausts. German antitank weapons from the Second World War. Crude, but reliable and effective. They had been carried by boys and women in the last months of the war, and many were the Russian tanks—not to mention a few American and British—they had destroyed. Each was capable of firing only once, so Bolan had purchased three of them.

He pulled the first one free of the canvas. The weapon was remarkably simple—just a tube about thirty inches long, fitted with a bomb at one end, a sight and trigger in the middle, and open at the rear.

Bolan had never fired a Panzerfaust, but he knew how it worked. The man at the machine gun was looking up at the bridge, apparently waiting for the command to fire, while the bullhorn continued to shriek. Bolan tucked the Panzerfaust under his arm, pulled the safety pin and raised the sight. The sight had apertures marked 30, 60 and 100 meters, and the foresight was nothing more than a pin that stuck up on the top of the bomb. He sighted through the 30-meter aperture and squeezed the trigger.

The Panzerfaust flashed and roared, and the bomb shot over the water, its fins unfolding as soon as they were out of the tube. Designed to pierce tank armor, it easily penetrated the steel skin of the patrol boat. A kilo and a half of TNT/Cyclonite exploded amidships, just under the bridge. The boat shuddered; hatches popped open, smoke blowing out; loose equipment rattled to the deck; men shrieked.

Bolan tossed the expended Panzerfaust tube overboard and snatched up another one. Everything was confusion aboard the Libyan boat. Men scrambled through hatches onto the deck. The man with the bullhorn was screaming orders now. Bolan's eyes were on the machine gunner. He was taking aim, and suddenly the muzzle of the machine gun was alive with orange fire. Bolan squeezed away the second bomb, aiming a little higher. The bomb hit above the deck, penetrated the main cabin and exploded inside. The machine gunner was blown over the rail and dropped to the main deck. One leg of the radar tripod broke, and the boat's fire-control radar crashed onto the bridge. The bullhorn fell silent.

Smoke poured out of a hatch amidships. Sailors raced wildly around the decks in panic. Bolan threw the second tube into the sea and picked up the third Panzerfaust. He aimed his third shot at the hull toward the rear, thinking he could rupture the boat's fuel tanks and start a major fire. The bomb flew straight and fast. It burst through, exploded and tore a gaping hole in the hull. The force of the blast had been confined by the heavy machinery inside. The damage was above the waterline, but as the boat pitched, the hole plunged into the waves and let in a ton of salt water.

Bolan gunned the outboard and turned the stern of his rubber boat toward the Libyans. Someone was bound to open fire, and the warrior wanted to put distance between himself and the ship.

The Libyan vessel was taking on water through its ruptured stern and settling rapidly into the sea. Lifted high on a wave, Bolan saw the main deck awash. The sailors tossed rubber dinghies overboard and clambered down into them. Some men carried white bales of the type he'd left to be taken by the tide on the Syrian beach. Perhaps their personal fortunes in deadly narcotics.

A fiery explosion shook the attack boat. Shattered, it listed and slipped silently out of sight, leaving nothing behind other than half a dozen rubber dinghies grabbed at by swimming men.

The outboard drove Bolan's boat west. Cyprus was still four hours away.

3

Three days after he came ashore on Cyprus, Bolan was in France, keeping an appointment with Emily Grant. The news media went wild over the sinking of the Libyan gunboat, a few commentators approving, many more clucking over the risk some "cowboy" operation had entailed. Rampant speculation attributed the sinking to everyone from Israel to Indonesia. Most guesses had it that the United States was somehow involved, though no one could figure how the operation had been carried out. A few commentators spoke admiringly of "America's newfound ability to carry out a clandestine operation effectively, and so quietly it is possible the world will never learn how it was done."

"The government of the United States vehemently denies any knowledge," Emily said. "Much less any connection. Every government in Western Europe is shrieking denials that they had anything to do with it. Colonel Khaddafi is threatening an Islamic jihad, in which he promises he'll wipe out Washington and New York, plus maybe London and Paris, just for good measure, 'by the righteous indignation of the faithful everywhere.' He's also complaining at the UN, and wants the Security Council to condemn the United States for 'racist aggression' against an 'innocent third-world nation.'"

"Too bad the estimable colonel wasn't aboard the boat," Bolan murmured.

"Your name has been mentioned," she went on. "The French government made formal inquiry as to whether you had anything to do with it. The State Department replied that the government of the United States has never heard of you. The CIA, being a little more candid, assured the French that you weren't involved to the best of its knowledge."

"I think you're telling me some Libyan sailors survived the sinking of their boat."

"Two Libyan sailors, plus an Iranian and a Corsican. The latter two disappeared shortly after they were put ashore at Famagusta. The two Libyans swore their patrol boat was sunk by rockets fired by American jet aircraft, at least ten of them—of which the heroic Libyans shot down six and damaged two more. That's the official line from Libya. The French asked who was at sea in a rubber boat equipped with a sophisticated recoilless rifle—and where did he go. I wish we could tell them."

"I scuttled the rubber boat," Bolan told her. "Then I swam ashore with my kit. Strolled down the beach in a flowered shirt and a pair of shorts, camera slung over my shoulder—the stuff I'd carried in a waterproof pouch. Made myself look like a tourist."

Emily laughed and put her hand on his. "You lose your .44?" she asked.

He nodded. "And the Beretta, too. Left them in the rubber boat. As it turned out, the Cypriot customs officer didn't even look in my camera bag, but my cover would have been blown if he had. I couldn't risk it, though I regret losing the weapons. They're on the bottom, five miles off the coast. Uh, someone will replace them, I take it. I have a feeling I'm going to need them."

"What have you got now?" she asked.

He looked away from her for a moment, distracted by shrieks and laughter.

Bolan and the woman were in a dark, smoky nightclub in Le Lavandou, the Riviera town a few miles west of Saint-Tropez that had for many years escaped the worst manifestations of tourism and had remained a family-style resort, where knowledgeable travelers could enjoy the beach without the jingle-jangle of Nice, Cannes and Saint-Tropez.

The shrieking that had caught the warrior's attention came from two mud-wrestling girls, one of whom had just lost the fun spirit of the game and was screaming and throwing mud. It was a memorable sight: a naked girl covered in slimy brown mud from head to toe, trying to stand in the tub of wet, slippery slime, shrieking with frustration and fury, and slinging handfuls of mud at her hysterically laughing opponent. Naturally the mud was missing the laughing woman and went flying indiscriminately into the patrons at ringside tables. Happily, they were amused, not angry.

Bolan looked away from the muddy girls and turned his attention back to Emily, who was wearing what was inconspicuous in this place: a pair of skimpy, skin-tight shorts and a tight cotton T-shirt. Her belly and navel were bare between the waistband of the shorts and the loose end of the undersize shirt. The cotton stretched tight across her generous breasts, leaving little to the imagination.

"Speaking of pistols, Emily," Bolan began, "aren't you carrying one?"

She slipped her straw purse toward him under the table and opened it slightly to show him a little automatic nestled between a handkerchief and a wad of franc notes.

"I don't go around naked," she said wryly.

He grinned. "Just about. Any new developments."

She shrugged. "We know a little more. You did a good job, but you can't sink every Libyan gunboat in the Mediterranean from rubber rafts."

"It's not just the Libyans," Bolan explained. "There has to be somebody else behind what's going on. The Libyans didn't kill Perugio and Mendoza, if for no better reason than that they wouldn't have known who they were."

"Absolutely right," she agreed. "In fact, we have reason to think that Colonel Khaddafi—for all the cut he gets from the trade—is an unwilling participant. He lets them use his gunboats because he's scared to death."

"Of the real crazies?" Bolan suggested.

"Well, actually the crazies can defend themselves against their fellow crazies reasonably well. All they have to do is kill anyone they suspect. No, there's more to this whole scheme than that. While you've been out doing a brilliant job of taking out a boatload of morphine—plus, we think, a load of explosives destined for the Irish Republican Army—some less glamorous laborers in the vineyard have been doing some prosaic investigative work and have come up with a likely explanation of what's going on. I say 'likely.' We could be wrong.''

"I'm all ears."

"I suppose you've heard of Union Corse?" she asked.

"I've come across them a time or two."

"Friends of yours?"

"Well, not exactly," Bolan replied. "They're more along the lines of the organization I set out to destroy. It's the Corsican Mafia, and they've got what, a century of tradition? Two centuries?"

"Exactly," she said. "Corsica was once an Italian island, until the French took it two centuries ago. Napoléon was a Corsican. His family name was Bonaparte. His parents spoke Italian. When he went to the French West Point, Saint-Cyr, he was mocked as an Italian who spoke bad French. In fact, Napoléon always spoke French with a thick Italian accent. The man buried in Les Invalides was more Italian than French, though it pains the French to admit it. Anyway, Corsica, like Sicily, has always had its 'men of respect.' Only the Corsican Mafia, the Union Corse, has always been fiercer and smarter than the Sicilian Mafia, which is known as the Cosa Nostra in the States. To the dons of Union Corse, the Mafia in Italy is nothing but a gang of murderous grafters, and the Cosa Nostra is just an organization of American street muggers.''

"Wrong.''

Emily shrugged. "Sure, wrong. But in its own judgment, Union Corse is an aristocracy, looking down from a lofty viewpoint on the peasant street hoodlums of the Mafia and Cosa Nostra. Anyway, they are smarter and tougher. They went into the mountains and resisted the French two hundred years ago. They went into the mountains and held out against the Nazis during World War II. They like to think of themselves as an association of brave men, who live by their own rules, against anyone who tries to rule them. Unfortunately—''

"Unfortunately," Bolan interrupted, "that's just what the Sicilian Mafia likes to think. Anyway, you think Union Corse is behind this new heroin traffic?''

"We think so. That seems to be the problem—an alliance between the Muslim suppliers and Union Corse as the refiners and distributors.''

"That answers my question," Bolan told her. "I couldn't see how a gang of so-called Islamic fanatics, no matter how committed, could have the smarts to move in on the market in Europe and America. If the Corsicans are involved, it's a whole lot easier to understand. They'd know who Perugio and Mendoza were, as well as Dubois and Piombo. And torturing a man to death is right down their alley. It's a part of their noble tradition.''

"One hell of a dangerous alliance," Emily said, looking for a moment at the burly bartender who was trying to separate the mud wrestlers.

The two girls were slippery, and he couldn't find secure footing in their pool of mud. The crowd roared with laughter as he slipped and fell on his back in the mud. No doubt he was part of the act.

"Apart from the Golden Triangle," Emily continued, "the Shiites control the world's greatest source of opium—all the poppy fields of Iran and those of eastern Turkey. They can supply tons of morphine base, and the Union Corse has the resources to refine and move it. When the Corsicans move in on someone else's territory, too bad for that someone. They either stand aside or—"

"Or they're tortured to death as an example to others," Bolan finished.

"That's the way it's worked so far. They're moving more top-grade heroin into Western Europe and America than has ever been moved before. The number of addicts is growing at a phenomenal rate. We've talked about a heroin epidemic. This is growing into a full-scale plague. Not to mention cocaine. They're moving in on that, too. The Colombians think they're murderously tough? They might be, but with the Union Corse they're up against men just as ruthless. What's more, they might need two or three more centuries to develop the tough, shrewd, suspicious mentality that's second nature to those Corsicans."

"So we're supposed to take on the Union Corse and do whatever we have to do to plug the pipeline," Bolan surmised.

"Right. I've been assigned to work with you. Officially I'm supposed to be the 'head' of the team, but we work as partners."

"*Be* the head of the team," Bolan said. "It's okay with me. If Fox Den *thinks* it has a team working on this, I'd rather it think you are the head. Don't worry about it."

THEY HAD TAKEN only one room—less likely to be noticed, she had said, than a man and woman apart—in a modest pension in the village of Bormesles-Mimosas, on the hill above Le Lavandou. It was a second-floor room with a little balcony that overlooked the Mediterranean and Le Lavandou from the hillside. Pots of flowers flourished on the balcony, and flies flew in through the unscreened window.

One creaking brass bed with resisting springs and a thin mattress dominated the room, and there had been no question that they should sleep in it together; the question had remained as to what would happen when they were in bed side by side.

What happened was what was inevitable in the circumstances. It was natural, not contrived, with no need of rationalization, and both Bolan and Emily Grant were content and satisfied when they lay apart afterward, a little sweaty but comfortable, sipping sparingly from glasses of brandy.

"I don't understand you," he said to her. And he didn't. He had difficulty understanding why any beautiful, feminine young woman, who might have chosen almost any kind of life, should have elected to dedicate herself to a profession that wasn't just dangerous, but was also dull most of the time, as well as relentlessly demanding and fatiguing. "Why did you choose to get into this business?"

Emily set her glass on the small night table. "Why did you, Mack?"

"Personal reasons, at first," he said quietly. "I got a firsthand look at what the takers of this world to do innocent people."

"Well, same here."

He nodded, choosing not to press her. If she wanted to tell him, she would.

Emily sighed. "Bob doesn't know. I had a sister who got hooked on heroin. No accident. The pusher knew what he was doing—hooking another kid, creating a market for himself if nothing more, but...I imagine you know what happened next."

"I suppose he turned her out to support her habit."

"A common street hooker," she said bitterly. "Janice was nineteen years old. She looked forty-five. Some of the johns abused her, beat her. Eventually she OD'd. Or got a contaminated fix. You know what they use to cut the stuff. Anything they have handy, including roach poison. She died."

"I'm sorry, Emily."

"Yeah, so were the cops, the narcs and the D.A. 'Not enough evidence.' Okay. I prosecuted the pusher myself. With a .32 Colt."

"You're lucky they didn't—"

"Arrest me? They weren't any smarter about that than they were about any of the rest of it. They couldn't imagine the grieving little sister whacking a Colombian dealer."

Bolan nodded.

Emily reached for her glass. "I took out one small-time dealer. It felt good, but there were six guys glad to see him go. It gave them a chance to replace him. That's when I decided I had to go a different route if I really wanted to do something that would make a difference."

"It's like knocking off that Libyan gunboat," Bolan said. "It was spectacular, but how much difference will it really make? What do you want to bet I only managed to stop one shipment? Or maybe two or three. Anyway, how do they get the stuff ashore?"

"The Libyan gunboats don't enter European ports. They don't have to. Any given night there are a thousand boats off the coast of France, Spain and Italy— fishing boats, yachts, you name it. There's radar surveillance of the gunboats, but they put rubber boats over the side and transfer the morphine base. Any one of a thousand, coming in at dawn or a little after, could be carrying a delivery. Then it goes to a laboratory to be refined somewhere."

"The lab has to be here in southern France," Bolan said. "Has to be. Apart from some sort of tradition, it just makes all kind of sense."

"You wouldn't think so. Sûreté is tough. I mean, the French police—"

"The problem," Bolan interrupted, "is that drug trading doesn't come under the jurisdiction of GIGN, their antiterrorist unit. If the French saw it that way—"

"They'd move in and do what you and I are assigned to do."

Bolan leaned over Emily and kissed her full, cool lips. For a long time they lay quietly together, each lost in thought. Then the warrior switched off the light, and they drifted off to sleep.

In the morning they drove down to Le Lavandou in a tiny Simca Emily had rented in Nice. Bob Millard had driven in from Marseilles and was to meet them on the boardwalk near the beach.

Millard, as they had expected, lay on a wooden beach chair rented from his hotel. A pitcher of sangría sat on a little table by his chair, as well as three plastic glasses. He had already turned faintly pink in the sun though he had protected his balding head with a floppy white hat. His camera—Bolan knew, though it wasn't noticeable—wasn't a camera but a radio transceiver.

"I've been sent to worse place," Millard declared as the new arrivals sat down in the sand near where he lay.

Children played in the gentle surf, attended by barebreasted young mothers; yachts rolled easily on the waves a few hundred yards offshore; a bright yellow sun blazed down from a cloudless sky.

"Bob," Bolan said quietly, "what do we know?"

"A little. We think we know who runs the operation from the Corsican side. His name is Vittorio Muro. He's sixty-four years old. He's sometimes called *padrone*, though never to his face because he doesn't like it. His home is a villa in the Corsican hills above Murato. He has never been arrested, never charged with a crime, nor was his father, from whom he inherited most of his money and position. Most of what we know about him is rumor."

"I know who he is," Bolan said. "He financed a conspiracy to shoot down Air Force One when it was carrying the President to a summit conference. He provided the Egyptian pilot and the money they needed to buy the Russian interceptor that was to have made it look like the Soviets had assassinated the President. Yeah, I know something about Signor Muro."

"It's rumored that he's worth more than two billion francs—let's say two hundred and fifty million dollars, at least. He doesn't deposit his money in Swiss banks, he *owns* Swiss banks. The man has homes in France, Italy, Spain, Paraguay. He owns his own fleet of jet aircraft, based mostly at the airport in Poretta. He has a fleet of boats. Right now he's living on a 150-foot yacht backed up to the quay at Saint-Tropez. It's called *Santa Margherita*."

"He's a clever man," Bolan told them. "When the White Front conspiracy 'collapsed' all the chief conspirators died, one way or another. Muro's participation was so well concealed, no one could even prosecute him. I'd guess he's given up political conspiracy and gone back to what he knows best.''

"The rest of the story is that he can order anyone's death, by a word, by a flick of a finger," Millard continued. "And, apparently, he does."

"Well, he's missed some of us," Emily said. "Here we sit, and he has to know that people like the three of us are his sworn enemies."

"Officially—" Millard lifted his glass of sangría and took a small sip "—our government cares little about his criminal empire, which is based chiefly in Europe and the Middle East. He might not yet understand that we—"

"Have decided to kill him?" Bolan suggested.

"No." Millard put his glass aside and spoke firmly. "No, someone would inherit. His sons, maybe. Some lieutenant. Union Corse doesn't die with its chiefs. If we kill Muro, it will only cause a hiccup in the big operation. The point is to stop the operation. No single killing will stop that."

"Of course, if they thought their allies did it . . ." Emily ventured.

"Yes," Millard agreed. "Now you're talking. Make them distrust one another and the killing begins." He smiled. "Use our brains as well as our brawn."

"Where's the lab?" Bolan asked.

"That's the key," Millard admitted. "Our information is incomplete, but we think there's just one laboratory, where all the stuff is refined. Hit the lab and you hit where it hurts."

"And all you need to do is find out where it is," Emily said dryly.

"That's the deal, and that's your assignment. Find the lab. Knock it out."

"You're sure it's not on Corsica?" Bolan asked.

"Don't think so," Millard replied. "The padrone likes to keep his turf clean. He doesn't want his hills swarming with French troops. Anyway, transportation out of Corsica could become a problem. It's a small island. International naval forces could check every boat and plane leaving the island, effectively close their trade routes. No, we think the lab's somewhere in France, likely southern France—"

"More than likely, within fifty miles of here," Emily interrupted.

Millard nodded. "That's where the labs have usually been, not far from Marseilles. It's a source of the necessary supplies, and the heroin can go out over scores of routes—highways, by air, by sea, by train. Southern France swarms with tourists in summer. Any of them can be couriers."

"Truckloads of fish go to Paris every day," Emily commented.

"Plus wine, vegetables and fruits," Millard added. "Thousands of trucks, thousands of automobiles, hundreds of railroad cars, hundreds of planes, on their way to every city in Europe. And any handbag, any suitcase, any automobile... Well, you get the idea? What could be better for them? Who could check all that traffic?"

"So the raw stuff comes in from the Mediterranean," Bolan summarized, "is refined in a big lab somewhere in southern France, and then goes out into the channels of commerce—''

"In thousands of different ways," Millard finished. "And no one carrier knows where it came from. You know. College kids. They spend a vacation on the Riviera beaches and recover the cost of their vacation by carrying a little heroin back to Paris, or down to Rome, or up to Frankfurt. Not big-time crooks. Just kids interested in making a few bucks. Tourists from the States, willing to risk what they risk by carrying a kilo or two. The stuff goes inside spare tires, in the wheel wells of airplanes, in sailors' duffel bags, in the tool kits of railroad men, in the bellies of iced fish, in hollowed-out vegetables..."

"The lab," Emily said. "The source."

"The lab," Millard agreed. "It was a major achievement to sink the Libyan gunboat and whatever it was carrying, but it was just one shipment."

"The *Santa Margherita* would be clean, I imagine," Emily said.

"From the keel to the mast top," Millard replied. "Vittorio Muro would never risk having heroin found aboard his yacht. On the other hand, other yacht owners go out at night and meet the Libyan gunboats."

"They're blackmailed and threatened, right?" Bolan suggested.

"Right."

"So," Emily said, "the job is easy—find the secret lab, which they hide and guard by every means they know, break through its security and destroy it. While we're at it, we have to make Muro believe he's been betrayed."

"Or—just as good—make some people believe Muro has betrayed *them*," Millard told her.

"Easy enough," Emily deadpanned.

"Is our government going to supply the weapons?" Bolan asked.

"Your government is ready to supply money," Millard replied. He nodded toward a beach bag. "You'll find half a million francs in there. Plus documents. Forged, of course. From there you're on your own. Oh. There's one more thing." He nodded at Bolan. "There's a Walther in the car to replace your Beretta. You also said you lost your Desert Eagle but I couldn't get you another on such short notice. You know that's a very special weapon.

"Well, anyway," Millard continued. "The Walther's a damned fine weapon, Mack. Enjoy the sun while I go to the car and get it."

Millard walked back toward the car park that faced the sand. Bolan reached into the beach bag the agent had left. He tore open a corner of one of the packages in it and riffled through the franc notes. The half million was there, all right, as well as sets of passports, driver's licenses, credit cards, all the litter of official paper and bank plastic an ordinary tourist carried. The Den had—

The morning calm split thunderously with the violence of a murderous explosion. Smoke and flame roared up over the car park, which was filled with debris that had once been three or four vehicles. The air rang with screams.

Bob Millard had been blown to bits.

4

The *Santa Margherita* was a handsome yacht, one of the most admired on the Mediterranean. At first glance the big and obviously costly yacht backed to the quay at Saint-Tropez appeared to be a sailing vessel with two tall masts, but it was in fact diesel powered. It had a black hull with white trim, and the rigging was painted white, as well. The teak and oak of its cabins and decks were superbly finished. The orderly, utilitarian web of its stays and sheets spoke a seagoing language.

On a Saturday morning its crew was busy on the decks, scrubbing, polishing, hosing off the last trace of salt spray. Dressed in tight black pants and white shirts, they ranged from middle-aged, mustached men, obviously lifelong yacht sailors, to hard-looking types who probably knew where guns were within reach anywhere on the deck.

Mack Bolan sat at a table on the quay, sipping coffee. He was dressed as a tourist now: sunglasses, sun hat, T-shirt printed with the names Joe and Deirdre. The Walther pistol Bob Millard had meant to give him had disappeared in the explosion at Le Lavandou, probably thrown out over the water and lying in the shallow salt water off the beach. Buying a pistol in the south of France—particularly without identifying yourself to people you didn't want to know you—wasn't easy, but he and Emily had discreetly shopped around and had come up with a 9 mm Luger. It was an antique, manufactured in 1938 as a German officer's side arm. But this one was in good condition, and Bolan knew from experience that the Luger was deadly accurate and one-hundred-percent reliable. It lay in his camera bag, within easy reach.

The sun shone hazily high in a misty sky. The day was warm, though the likelihood of its becoming hot was suggested in the air. Bolan watched Emily. It was difficult to believe the woman would do what she meant to do. She was strolling along the quay, strumming on a guitar and singing.

Emily wore a brief white satin bikini under an open pink shirt; dark sunglasses covered her eyes; her feet were bare. Before she had left Bolan she'd made a point of smearing some street dust on her legs and arms, intending to look like one of the mercenary urchins who sold whatever a man might want on the Saint-Tropez waterfront. Beautiful though the quay was, it was also a meat market.

She was only one of half a dozen attractive girls who walked up and down the quay, singing, strumming guitars, not expecting to live off the coins tourists tossed at them but hoping to be noticed by the men on the yachts, to be asked aboard, to become, however briefly, the used but pampered girl-playthings aboard those boats. Some of them made a year's income in just one night.

Occasionally one was set for life after a "pleasure" cruise.

Of course, there was another side to it. Some girls invited aboard these big boats suffered horribly at the hands of these millionaires—Arabs, Argentines, Germans, Italians, occasionally an American. A few girls came ashore with enough money to buy a Maserati and speed to Paris. Occasionally one was thrown overboard at sea. It was straightforward commerce, with its rewards and risks well understood. The gawking tourists who tossed coins never imagined what was going on.

Emily had hoped to be invited aboard the *Santa Margherita* if she made it plain enough that that was what she wanted—and if she made it plain enough what she offered. She was, after all, a beautiful, seductive young woman. Bolan had objected to her method of gaining entry. He had insisted he would get aboard by posing as an unemployed yacht sailor. She'd replied that there were too many of those on the quays—and, anyway, what could a sailor learn as a foredecks crewman of *Santa Margherita*? If he so much as saw the padrone, he would be lucky. But she, she would be invited into the main cabin. She would see what no sailor even guessed at.

Bolan hoped she would fail.

Emily didn't intend to fail. She carried a tiny package of plastique taped out of sight inside the guitar. It was a small amount, but enough to blow a hole in the waterline of the *Santa Margherita* or blow a man to hell from his bed. In the lining of the guitar case she had three slender blades, each razor sharp, each capable of slitting a man's throat or his body from belly to balls. She knew how to use her weapons. She was capable of killing without them, too, using her hands. Emily Grant was one formidable woman.

Emily had grown up in Minneapolis. To stroll the Saint-Tropez waterfront, exhibiting herself like a whore, was the antithesis of everything her Lutheran parents had taught her. Yet, she knew, they would endorse her purpose: to avenge her sister, of course, but far more important than that, to prevent the entry into the United States of tons of heroin. Her parents' morals, like hers, were large, capable of putting the petty behind the important; and if she had to play the whore to destroy a vicious commerce, they wouldn't censure her.

"Mademoiselle."

Ah, good. A thin, dark man on the stern above her looked down and spoke.

"Monsieur?"

"Would you care to play and sing for the gentleman who owns this yacht while he has his breakfast?"

"I should be honored."

The breakfast room, in the stern cabin, with broad windows overlooking the quay, was light and airy. A table was set with white linen, silver, a single pink rose in a crystal vase. The fragrance of fresh-ground, fresh-brewed coffee steamed from the spout of a silver pot. A white-jacketed chef stood ready to serve from his warming table as soon as the master of the yacht arrived.

"Sit down there, *mademoiselle*, and wait."

A moment later Vittorio Muro walked in. He glanced at her, smiled, then turned his attention to his table, inspecting what was offered, and how it was laid out, with a critical eye.

Two men dressed in black suits accompanied the padrone to his breakfast table. He himself wore black trousers and a white golf shirt. Muro was only sixty-four years old, but the deep wrinkles in his tanned face suggested a man of eighty. His eyes were light blue and watery, his hair gray. With the practiced air of a man who was accustomed to the attention of servants, he allowed his attendants to pull out his chair and to push it back as he seated himself. Emily had never before seen a man with such a confident patrician air. He glanced at the table setting and at the small pile of newspapers waiting for him. He drew a deep breath.

"*Signorina*," he said quietly to Emily, "I heard your singing from my cabin."

Emily nodded cautiously. He spoke English to her, and she wished he hadn't. He had already guessed, apparently, that she was an American.

"Your name is . . ."

"Linda Williams."

"From?"

"Houston, Texas."

"And you are . . . ?"

She shrugged and smiled shyly. "A student, I guess. My family absolutely insists I come home at the end of the summer, so I suppose I'll go back to my studies at the University of Texas—"

"Austin?" he asked.

"Yes, sir. Austin," she replied, disturbed to hear that he knew where the university was. He knew more about the States than she had imagined, which would make everything more difficult. More dangerous. "Two years ago. I've been wandering around Europe since—"

"I understand," he said. "But you are a bit over-dressed for my taste, *signorina*. Do you mind?"

His meaning was obvious. She unhooked her bikini top and put it aside, on her guitar case.

"Ah," he breathed, his eyes caressing her naked breasts. "Yes. You are beautiful. If you stay aboard, I will expect you to be unclothed at certain times. I am an old man and take my pleasure where I can. It pleases me to gaze at beautiful women. Would you like to stay on board?"

"I . . . I think so," she replied. "I think I would like that very much."

"We will of course make it worth your while."

"Thank you. I hoped . . . Well, you understand."

"Yes, I do understand. Now then, Linda. While I have my breakfast, will you play and sing for me? Put the shirt aside, too, my sweet. I don't want anything to interfere with my looking at your lovely body. American girls have so much more interesting shapes than the French. I pride myself on being something of a connoisseur of breasts. For some reason, American girls have the most splendid ones. Texas girls especially. Maybe it's something about Texas, hmm? Everything is bigger in the state of Texas."

WHEN EMILY DIDN'T RETURN to the quay Bolan grew first impatient, then concerned. He couldn't remain around the stern of the *Santa Margherita*, conspicuously staring at it. He had other things to do, and she was supposed to be able to take care of herself.

It was pointless to try to discover who had blown away Bob Millard. His chief concern, and Emily's, was that whoever had done it might have been watching—perhaps with powerful binoculars from some distant window—and seen them meeting with Millard on the beach. He and Emily had talked about it and concluded it was unlikely that that final meeting with Bob had been watched. If it had been, surely the murder of Bob Millard would have been followed shortly by an attempt on their lives—which so far hadn't happened.

It was typical behavior of the Shiites to plant a bomb and distance themselves from it. They didn't care who died in their blasts, here any more than they cared about who died in Beirut.

Bolan and Emily had heard nothing from Fox Den, not that they expected to. There was no way they could be contacted except personally, by an agent who would recognize one of them, and that agent would have to travel to France. What was more, there were very few agents who *could* recognize them. He and Emily wouldn't have survived long if many people knew their faces.

Actually hers was memorable. But she varied her appearance, she'd told him, by changing her hairstyle, changing its color, wearing different makeup, changing her style of dress, and, above all, speaking different languages. A man who was certain he recognized her was almost invariably cut off when he heard her speaking a new language, not the one he'd heard her speak before. In Europe she spoke French most of the time. She wasn't often recognized as an American.

They had taken rooms at the Byblos Hotel, the best in Saint-Tropez, a sort of villa spread over a hillside above the town. He went back there for lunch. He might as well; apparently Emily wasn't going to leave the *Santa Margherita* any time soon.

He sat at a table near the pool, ostensibly playing the American tourist by scanning the *Herald-Tribune*. The explosion on the beach at Le Lavandou was the lead story. A woman and child had been killed in the explosion of Bob Millard's car, and the French government had lodged a complaint with Washington. They identified Millard as an American intelligence agent and implied that the United States was somehow responsible for the deaths of the woman and child—apparently on the theory that Millard had carelessly got himself murdered at the edge of a crowded beach and so had caused the deaths of innocents.

"Monsieur..." The woman who stood beside Bolan was eye catching. A dozen models were staying in the hotel. A crew of photographers was using Saint-Tropez as the background for the pictures that would become the illustrations for millions of dollars worth of fashion-magazine advertising during the coming months. The girls were being photographed in next spring's fashions, in swimsuits and in lingerie, some of them posing around the pool. Bolan and Emily had been

amused yesterday afternoon when they arrived, watching a cameraman underwater in the pool, using an Aqua-lung so he could stay down, while two models tried bravely to hold their breath and pose and smile, one in a bikini, the other, for some odd reason, fully dressed in skirt, blouse, jacket, shoes and stockings. Each time the dressed one surfaced, a man had knelt at poolside to work on her makeup and to comb out her hair. The girl who had just spoken to Bolan was the one who had spent an hour fully dressed in that cold water.

"*Mademoiselle...?*"

"May I sit down with you, *monsieur?*" she asked. "For a moment?"

"Of course."

The woman was quite tall and slender, and had that long, bony face that high fashion modeling traditionally demands. She wore tight pink pants and a white knit shirt. Her makeup was extraordinary: vivid red and black, heavily applied. Dramatic. There was no question about that.

"I am grateful, *monsieur*," she replied. "To sit with you is the easiest way to avoid some... unwanted attention."

Bolan glanced around. An Arab in a flashy double-breasted suit stared at him, conspicuously annoyed.

"Put your hand on mine, *mademoiselle*," Bolan suggested. "And laugh."

She played along. "Ah, *monsieur*." She laughed again, this time naturally, not forcing it. "You are clever. My name is Yvette Duclos."

"I'm Joseph Robinson."

"Ah, yes. I noticed you here yesterday, with..."

"I noticed you, too. I hope you were well paid for what you were doing."

She smiled. "Of course. Would I have done so foolish a thing otherwise? Holding my breath under ice-cold water?"

"We all do foolish things for money," Bolan said dryly. "Would you like a drink or some lunch?"

"Thank you. You are, of course, American?"

"Yes. I am, of course, American. And you are, of course, French."

Yvette laughed yet again. "Of course." Her accent was light, only enough to add interest to her speech. "Would you order for me one of those American cocktails, a martini? Then, when it is here, taste it and tell me if it is good, then tell me how to make it?"

When the martini was brought, the Arab stalked into the hotel. That, too, amused Yvette. She sat with Bolan for an hour and drank two martinis while nibbling sparingly on some shrimp salad. He enjoyed her conversation but was glad when he could break away from her and return to the quay. Emily was nowhere to be seen.

Bolan returned to the Byblos, the only place she would know to contact him. He reserved a table for dinner and sat down in the dining room at eight.

"You are alone, Joseph?" Yvette said from behind him.

He nodded. "It seems that I am."

"Then...?"

"Of course. Are you still being pursued by that irritating Arab?"

"I think he has given up," she replied as she sat in the chair he had pulled out for her. "Anyway, I came looking for you. I am the envy of the other girls, to have been befriended by the handsome American."

Bolan smiled. "If that old gang of mine could only see me now."

Yvette Duclos was even more striking this evening. Her hair was bound so tightly behind her head that he wondered if she could close her eyes. Her makeup was as dramatic as before. Big dark eyes settled on him with a look of comfortable amusement. She wore a full skirt of shiny black silk, matched by a wide-shouldered jacket. Under the jacket her black silk blouse was so sheer that her breasts were visible whenever she allowed the jacket to gape.

"Tell me something, Joseph," she said when their dinner and wine were on the table. "Where is that beautiful American girl who was with you yesterday?"

"Found herself what we might call a berth on a yacht, I suspect."

"Then she's not...? I mean, you two aren't, uh, paired?"

"Not permanently," he answered.

"Ah. And do you, Joseph, think of yourself as a sophisticate?"

He shook his head. "I think of myself as a pretty straightforward guy."

"Straightforward," she mused. "Then I suppose you wouldn't happen to have—I mean, be able to supply a girl with—a pinch of feelgood dust?"

That caught the warrior's attention. "Coke? Sorry."

"Ah, well. We can do without it. I mean, I was thinking, if I came to your room, you might be able to supply... I mean, only a little. Only a line."

"Afraid not. Of course, if you want to come to my room anyway..." First the contrived meeting, now this. Bolan wondered what the woman was up to.

She grinned. "Of course. All the other girls would laugh at me if I failed to get that invitation."

BOLAN LEFT THE ROOM on the pretense of having left his credit card in the restaurant. He waited in the hallway for a few moments, then eased open the door to the room, which he'd left ajar. Yvette knelt on the floor, going through his suitcase.

In an instant he was on her, astonished to find himself thrown off by an expertly applied hold that rolled him painfully aside as Yvette scrambled to her feet. She grabbed for her purse—going for a gun, he figured. He lunged, tackled her around the ankles and brought her down hard.

"I could knock you out," he growled. "I doubt you've got a hold that will stop that."

She blew out an angry, frustrated breath and shrugged in surrender. "Open my purse," she demanded. "You should look at my identification."

He reached for her bag and opened it. She had a weapon in the purse, as he'd guessed. And an identity card with her photograph on it. Yvette Duclos, Police Judiciare, Service Régional de Provence. She was a cop.

As he squinted over the identity card, Yvette sat up. "All right, Joseph?"

He nodded and handed her the purse, pistol and card. "To what do I owe the honor?"

Yvette scrambled to her feet, then sat on the edge of the bed, rubbing her hip where she'd fallen when he tackled her. "I could say you owe it to the fact that you have a pistol in your camera bag," she said. "Of course, I didn't know that when I sought you out."

"Am I under arrest for something?"

"No, I don't think so. Not, anyway, if you tell me the truth."

"You haven't asked a question."

"What is your name?" she asked.

"Joseph Robinson."

Yvette shook her head. "Don't play— What is it you Americans say? Don't play games with me? I think I know who you are. And if so, you and I might be working on the same thing. It would be absurd to do otherwise."

"Well, who do you think I am?"

"I think you are Mack Bolan, and I think you are here because Vittorio Muro is here. I think the American girl is another agent and has done something so foolish I can hardly believe you allowed it."

5

The "Arab" was Maurice Grimmaud, another agent of Police Judiciare, the police force responsible for fighting crime throughout France. Sûreté is really just an administrative office; it is the PJ that has thousands of policemen on the streets and is chiefly responsible for enforcing the laws of France.

"All of you are police agents?" Bolan asked.

"No, not at all," Inspector Grimmaud replied. They were sitting in Bolan's room at three in the morning. "The camera crew knows who Yvette is. The other models do not."

"It amuses them to give me ridiculous assignments like going into the water fully and formally clothed," Yvette sniffed.

Yvette was, as she and Grimmaud explained, actually a mannequin—an experienced professional high-fashion model—much in demand by couturiers. Grimmaud mentioned to Bolan a number of advertising campaigns that had featured her as the clotheshorse; but Bolan had to admit he hadn't seen them. As she traveled in France, modeling clothes, she was often approached by dealers in cocaine, heroin and other illegal substances. Her status as a model had been valuable to Police Judiciare.

"I must have disappointed you when I told you I had no coke," Bolan said.

Yvette smiled. "I would have been disappointed if you had."

Inspector Grimmaud wasn't actually an Arab. He was an Algerian Muslim, able to pose as an Arab when necessary. His brother and sister had died from drug overdoses, and he was a dedicated enemy of every trader in narcotics; his only wish was to bring them all to justice.

"We know who you are," Grimmaud told him. "We want you to work with us."

"I work alone."

Yvette smiled. "So we have been told. Who, then, is the lovely Emily Grant?"

They knew too much—his name, Emily's, the relationship between them. The French had a reputation for effective, in fact ruthless, police work. "I've worked with Emily for a few days," he said. "Still, I work alone."

"Not in France," Grimmaud replied bluntly. "Not in this affair."

"Your government has denied you exist," Yvette said. "Still, it has sent you to use your particular methods to interrupt the new flow of heroin and cocaine into European and American markets. We have as much interest in that as you do. If we work separately, we can interfere with each other. Together..."

"Your government," Bolan said, "seems to think it was our fault that Millard was killed. That's a little off base, isn't it?"

"My new friend," Yvette protested, "do you really suppose the insane mouthings of our socialist president mean anything? Even he fully understands that they do not. He makes pro forma protests, to salve the sensitive international consciences of his political associates, then he sends us orders to do what we must do. You sank the Libyan gunboat. I am sure it was you. Monsieur le Président clucks, shakes his head and protests. But if he could see you in private, he would shake your hand."

"The world is full of idiots," Grimmaud added. "But not all who sing from their song sheets—or march in the streets with their banners—are idiots, too. We all make our political concessions and do what we must."

This had been Bolan's experiences before: the French could be supremely pragmatic. They were, in fact, the world's leading pragmatists—capable of quietly strangling the same "freedom fighter" they were publicly proclaiming as a hero. By the same token, they would strangle *him*, if they decided it was in the national self-interest.

"So you have it figured out, have you?" Bolan asked.

"The same way you have it figured out," Yvette replied. "The Corsicans are working with the Shiites. They've rid the world of some of its worst scum, but only to take over the scum's businesses for themselves."

"Do they know you?" Bolan asked.

Grimmaud shook his head. "No. We are confident of that. That's why we are here. And we are confident they don't know you. They know your name and reputation, but they don't know your face."

"You'd be dead if they did," Yvette said. "They never hesitate to kill."

"Then how about Emily?" Bolan asked.

"Stupid!" Yvette hissed. "How long can she stay aboard the *Santa Margherita* before they learn who she is? Anyway, what value is there in planting herself aboard Vittorio Muro's yacht? We know who he is and what he does. What we need to know is the location of the laboratory."

"Wherever it is, it's behind a wall of security," Bolan told them. "That's the point. Find a place that's heavily guarded. How well can they conceal their defense arrangements?"

"Quite well," Grimmaud replied. "Let there be no doubt. Do you suppose we haven't been looking?"

"And you're good," Bolan admitted. "Can you accept my methods?"

"*We* can," Yvette said. "Our government can't—in the official sense, anyway. But then, does your government accept you, officially?"

"We don't need to talk about that."

"It's a question of humanity," Yvette stated. "You are fortunate that we French know how to place that consideration above all others."

"The lab," Bolan said. "Don't you have any leads?"

Grimmaud shook his head. "It has to be within a hundred kilometers of here. A hundred and fifty at the very most." He shrugged. "That covers a lot of territory—mountains, hills, forests, coastline, major cities..."

"Boats."

"Thousands of them. If we identified a dozen, still we wouldn't know much. We'd have to follow a shipment all the way. They know that. No one courier knows the destination of the next. And they use— what?—five or six between the rendezvous at sea and the laboratory. With security precautions at each transfer."

"Which means," Bolan observed, "that Emily's venture aboard the *Santa Margherita* isn't so stupid after all."

EMILY HAD BEGUN to think she'd made a mistake. Vittorio Muro was a formidable man—long-experienced, shrewd, cautious and perceptive. He enjoyed every pleasure: the best of food and wine; redolent Cuban cigars that scented the cabins of the yacht with smoke that was almost a perfume; a small on-board library of the best in recent literature in three languages; distinguished music played through a high-fidelity sound system that brought a concert hall into the boat's main lounge; the attention of two beautiful young women, of whom Emily was one; dinner conversation that suggested nothing of the kind of business that might have produced the money that afforded the padrone all these luxuries. Everything was savored with the calm insouciance of an aristocrat quite used to the good life.

"I have been surprised," he said, "by the way the American wine makers have achieved such quality in so little time. We in Europe have cultivated our grapes for centuries, only to see the viniculture of California overtake most of our great wines in half a century. The best American doesn't approach the best French or Italian wine. Still, the everyday American wine is superior to the everyday French or Italian."

He enjoyed all his luxuries in moderation, Emily noted to her surprise. When he summoned her to his cabin late that first evening, she found him courteous, thoughtfully concerned for her feelings, interested in her background.

Indeed, she and the other woman, Barbara, might have been his daughters if not for the fact that he required both of them to go about the boat either naked or topless, except when they were on deck. That was the only evidence of their status. Otherwise, they ate at the padrone's table, enjoyed his music, were welcome to read his books and were treated by the crew with a deference second only to that accorded to Vittorio Muro himself.

For all she could tell, he was just an extremely wealthy man, enjoying a visit to the resort town of Saint-Tropez, aboard his unbelievably beautiful yacht. She saw no evidence that he was the leading padrone of Union Corse.

If there was evidence, it was perhaps in the closed and locked radio room amidships. There—from the look of the antennae mounted on the masts—the *Santa Margherita* could be in contact with the world.

She looked at the men who worked as Vittorio's crew and servants. All of them seemed simple enough. Were any armed? Who was his bodyguard? A man called Vergio, who dressed completely in black—black knit shirt, black trousers, black shoes—seemed to serve as the padrone's secretary and treasurer; but obviously he carried no gun under the knit shirt; neither did any other member of the crew.

Emily had free time. She joined Barbara in the lounge on the stern, where they could sip wine, listen to music and watch the traffic on the Saint-Tropez quay. Barbara was British, a shop girl who had sold expensive toiletries at Penhaligon in Wellington Street and had learned the speech patterns and mannerisms of the wealthy. She had dark brown hair and blue eyes, a faulted Oxonian accent and an all too conspicuous anxiety to earn as much money as she could as quickly as she could. After the summer, she told Emily, she would probably return to Penhaligon and ask for her job back.

"How long have you been aboard, Barbara?" Emily asked.

"Two weeks. And it's something of a record. Usually he gets bored within the week."

"I never heard his name before I came here. What's he into, oil?"

"Wish I knew," Barbara replied. "I'd put a few quid in it meself."

"Better we don't ask, hmm?"

The British girl shrugged. "I suppose. Not our problem, hey?"

Emily nodded. "Not our problem."

Evidence of the problem finally arrived on Emily's second night aboard the *Santa Margherita*. After a distinguished dinner the padrone suddenly dismissed the two young women who had sat on each side of him at the table. He was courteous but firm. They were to go to their cabins; he would call them later.

Emily went to her cabin. Vergio, she noticed with a pretense of casualness, followed her along the passage and saw that she had done what the padrone had ordered.

She sat on her berth for five minutes then checked her door. Vergio hadn't locked her in, as she had supposed he might. Emily slipped out, crept along the corridor and climbed the companionway to the main deck.

Saint-Tropez was beautiful in the moonlight. The quay was alive with reveling couples. People ate their dinners in waterfront restaurants, drinking wine and eating bouillabaisse, laughing and singing and anticipating. The yachts—none as big as the *Santa Margherita*—rolled gently on a swell driven by a cool breeze that came in from the Mediterranean. The air hung heavy with the smell of the tide.

Obedient to the rules established for her—since she didn't know who she might encounter or what excuse she might make for having left her cabin—Emily wore the bottoms of her white satin bikini. That left nowhere to carry a weapon, and she was apprehensive of what she might encounter on the deck of the yacht.

She sneaked to the stern and looked down at the quay, thinking she might see Bolan there. He was nowhere in sight. A strolling tourist stopped short when he caught sight of the topless woman. She retreated hastily.

Emily padded barefoot along the starboard side of the yacht. She peered into the lounge, through the windows that opened on the deck—it was deserted. She worked her way along, looking in each window. Nothing. Whatever Vittorio Muro was up to, he wasn't doing it where he could be seen from the windows that opened onto the deck.

His private cabin, to which she had been summoned the previous night, had portholes only on the hull. Emily stood at the rail, just above those portholes, and looked down. Could she . . . ?

It was possible.

Emily untied a mooring line that held the yacht in place at the quay and let it fall to the water. She glanced around then seized the loose line in both hands and swung herself over the rail. The line afforded her the means to lower herself down the black hull silently to just above the waterline. Her feet touched the cold water when she had a view through the porthole that opened into Muro's elegant cabin. Clinging to the rough hemp line, Emily peered into the cabin at a meeting already underway.

No surprise. It was what she had expected. Vittorio Muro was sequestered with a pair of mustached, swarthy men, both of whom carried pistols at their hips. They were either Shiites or Palestinians. In any event they were the kind she had expected—men carrying weapons they didn't need, men with the look of fanaticism burning in their eyes.

She couldn't hear what was being said. Vergio stood nervously at the door of Muro's cabin. The padrone sat at his antique desk, puffing calmly on a cigar and discoursing quietly with the two men. The thick glass of the porthole didn't allow a sound of their conversation to pass through.

Since she couldn't hear, Emily could see no point in hanging around. She clambered up and over the rail to the deck.

"Signorina." A crewman had rounded a corner from the port side. *"Che cosa significa questo?"*

He grabbed Emily's wrist and dragged her toward the companionway, then down to Muro's cabin. Vittorio appeared at the crewman's sharp rap, and she couldn't catch a word of their conversation. Whether the man had seen her climb over the rail, she didn't know.

"Linda," Vittorio said reproachfully, "did I not tell you to go to your cabin?"

"Yes, *signor*," she replied. "But not that I had to stay there. I had no idea I would offend you if I went on deck for some air and to look at the moon."

"Well, we will talk of it later. In the meanwhile, a little discomfort must be suffered to be sure you do not leave your cabin without permission." He smiled at her, a mysterious smile that didn't tell her if he had guessed she was a spy. "You will forgive us. We must assure ourselves of our privacy when we transact business."

His "little discomfort" was a set of leg irons, like oversize handcuffs, locked on her ankles. The sailor put them on after he accompanied her to her cabin. And he locked her door. She sat on the edge of her berth for a few minutes, looking at the shackles that impeded her movements; then, it being impossible to do anything more, she lay back and stared at the ceiling.

Emily had an idea about how to get out of the leg irons; she had escaped from handcuffs before. But if she slipped these shackles the padrone would know for sure that she was something other than a waterfront girl who'd come aboard to entertain him and earn some money; and that would be the end of her mission, given up before she could ferret out any useful intel. She turned on her side with a little difficulty and tried to go to sleep. Tomorrow was another day.

6

"We will not advise our superiors that you are working with us," Yvette Duclos said to Bolan. "May we assume you will not advise yours?"

Bolan shrugged. "You may assume that."

They were sitting at breakfast beside the pool at the Byblos. They had agreed—she, Bolan and Grimmaud—that it would be well to continue the impression they had already established: that the model Yvette and the American who called himself Robinson had begun sleeping together and that the Arab—Grimmaud's alter ego—was annoyed. So Grimmaud sat at another table, feigning irritation.

After breakfast Yvette returned to her work, posing at the edge of the pool in a black-and-white wraparound swimsuit. Bolan watched for a few minutes, then went to the car he and Emily had brought from Le Lavandou. The warrior had intended to explore the countryside around Saint-Tropez. He had some ideas about how to find the laboratory.

He and Emily had turned in the Simca and rented a BMW, thinking that for the work they might have to do they had better have something a little more powerful and a great deal faster. The BMW was parked in the hotel garage. Remembering what had happened to Millard, he examined the vehicle closely before he opened the door. But the car was clean. In fact, as he began to suspect, his new French acquaintances had thoroughly inspected the BMW already that morning. Inspector Grimmaud—or one of his men—had examined this car meticulously. Bolan knew the little signs— tiny scratches, clean spaces in the dust that usually lay thick on door sills and dashboards, and fingerprint smudges on windows and dials.

The French had done him another service. In the car, hidden under blankets on the floor in back, he found a pair of powerful binoculars, a silenced pistol of Finnish manufacture and a Beretta submachine gun.

The Finnish pistol was a Lahti M-35, a beautifully designed and manufactured 9 mm automatic. He'd learned to appreciate this weapon some time ago; a Lahti was what the British had issued him during a mission in the recent past. The sleek black pistol looked something like a Luger, but was very different, being machined to exceptionally close tolerances and assembled by hand to high standards to assure the Finnish army that their officers' side arm would function reliably in extreme cold, dust and mud. Bolan had given it that kind of test—extreme cold and wet—and it had functioned perfectly.

He knew that because of the hand craftsmanship used in its manufacture, it was an expensive pistol. The sound suppressor—which was a more accurate term than silencer—would reduce its muzzle crack to a hard grunt.

The Beretta Model 12 was something else—a cheap, rugged burp gun, capable of firing over five hundred 9 mm rounds a minute. It was a killer, plain and simple, with a long magazine hanging between its fore and aft grips. The sight and heft of it made the warrior regret all the more the loss of his own Beretta 93-R.

The binoculars were a welcome touch. He drove up around the hill, to the citadel above Saint-Tropez, from which he had a view of the yacht basin. Playing the tourist, he focused the glasses on the luxury vessels lying in the hazy sunlight of the basin far below—particularly, of course, on the *Santa Margherita*, the queen of the quay.

He spotted Emily, dressed in the shiny white bikini she'd been wearing when she went aboard the yacht the previous day.

She sat at a table on the rear deck, with coffee and croissants before her, conversing—apparently amiably—with a tanned, wizened man who shrugged often as he talked with her and seemed neither grim nor especially excited. Bolan tried to study her face. As far as he could tell, she was calm. Emily lifted her cup and sipped coffee as he adjusted the focus of the binoculars and tried to read her face. The man picked up a newspaper, glanced at it and seemed to make some remark about what he'd read. It was a peaceful, somewhat domestic scene.

Bolan drew a deep breath, immeasurably relieved. He could see no sign of anything being wrong. Apparently she had insinuated herself aboard the yacht and into the good graces of— Well, he had to suppose the dark man with the lined face was Vittorio Muro. He'd seen a blurred, black-and-white photograph of the *padrone*, and this man could very well be him.

Bolan scanned the decks of the *Santa Margherita*, looking for hardmen, for weapons. If they were there— and he was sure they were, somewhere—they were well concealed. The crew working around the decks seemed unarmed and had the appearance of typical sailors. Studying the yacht, Bolan noticed the array of antennae atop the center cabin and in the rigging. Otherwise, the handsome big yacht carried radar and a weather station—nothing out of the ordinary.

He looked again at Emily and Muro. Their conversation seemed a little more animated now, but not unfriendly. She was speaking emphatically, and the man was nodding. He laughed.

There was something about Emily, though . . . in the way she sat, unnaturally stiff. Bolan peered hard, taking in every detail. Then he saw that her ankles were chained together. No one on the quay could have noticed the shackles on her legs; from the quay they were below the rail and out of sight; but Bolan's position and the powerful binoculars enabled him to see the steel circles around her ankles and the half-dozen links of chain connecting them.

He stared at her face, puzzled. She was smiling. More than that, she was laughing. And the man remained calm, glancing back and forth from her to his newspapers, smiling, too, and chatting. The absence of tension was beyond explanation. How could she be smiling? Something was wrong. Not just a little wrong. Very wrong.

There was no way he could get aboard the *Santa Margherita*. Not in daylight anyway, and probably not even on a moonless night. The only way aboard the yacht, he judged, was through the laboratory somewhere in southern France. If Bolan judged his man correctly, nothing but big trouble would move Vittorio Muro to venture off his yacht and go ashore. When the padrone went ashore, he would either bring Emily with him or he would leave her with half the crew on board. A dramatic rescue was out of the question.

However innocent they looked, those sailors had to be soldiers of the Union Corse. The odds against overcoming all of them were great. Vittorio Muro and his guards had to be lured off the yacht.

BOLAN SPENT much of the rest of the day driving the roads behind the coastal highway, stopping often to scan the wooded hillsides with the binoculars. Reason and instinct combined to suggest to him that the shipments of morphine base came ashore on one of two stretches of coast: between Cannes and Toulon or between Montpellier and Narbonne. The French coast stretched from the Italian frontier at Menton to the border with Spain at Port Bou. Not all of it, though, was suitable for the traffic. Along the Cannes/Nice/Monte Carlo coast, the crowds were too great, the police too thick. West of Sète the roads were too few, too easily blocked. To the west, along the mosquito beaches, backed by marshes, tourists weren't so plentiful that strangers escaped notice. Here, he thought, between Cannes and Toulon, conditions were perfect for smuggling in the poison.

Here the tourists swarmed, but over a far longer coastal stretch, on kilometer after kilometer of shoreline, some of it beach, some rocky. Even at the height of the season, privacy could be found. Still, the traffic was so great that no one was conspicuous who didn't want to be. Scores of roads wound into the forested hills behind the Riviera coast. A car or van carrying morphine base could choose hundreds of routes to a laboratory in the hills. After the stuff was refined, the cars or vans going on to Paris and beyond had a choice of dozens of routes to the north—or they could go to Italy or Spain, using any number of roads.

France still had, in much of its territory, what Americans called boonies—deep river valleys, forests, hills, modest farms, even rough country over which a man on a horse would be hard put to travel. Paris wasn't all of France, any more than New York City was all of America.

So a day spent driving the hills behind the coast didn't produce a single lead. The warrior had suspected it wouldn't. He had done it more for the sake of his nerves than for any real expectation. Anyway, he had a better perspective on the problem.

At dinner with Yvette in the Byblos dining room, he told her about seeing Emily.

"They've got her legs chained, and she was acting as if nothing was wrong. I wonder if she's been drugged."

"I have more bad news for you in that respect," Yvette said. "Have you looked at the yacht basin this evening? Did you see what's happened? The *Santa Margherita* is gone. It went to sea late this afternoon."

THE SEA WAS EASIER to search than the wooded hills. Bolan didn't believe the yacht had gone far, only out to a rendezvous with a Libyan naval vessel.

When he insisted he would rent a boat and go, Yvette insisted that she accompany him. It would attract less attention, she said—a moonlight boat ride off the coast, man and woman; and, in any event, she could almost certainly obtain a boat at night, whereas he probably couldn't, since he was ostensibly an American tourist who likely wouldn't know how to handle a boat safely after dark. She, using her credentials as an agent of the Police Judiciare, could get the cooperation he would not.

They pushed off from the rental dock before nine o'clock, carrying hampers that looked as if they were filled with food and wine—one of them actually containing pistols, ammunition and half a dozen grenades. The other hamper held a radio transceiver and a portable radar device that might help them locate the *Santa Margherita*.

Bolan wore dark clothes as did Yvette. Once they were away from the quay and out of sight, she pulled a Beretta automatic from one of the hampers, shoved in a magazine and chambered a round.

The Police Judiciare had been in contact with the French naval base at Toulon regarding the whereabouts of the *Santa Margherita*, and had been told the big yacht was cruising slowly to the east, some twenty-five kilometers offshore. By midnight it would likely be off the coast of Nice. The outboard-powered launch Yvette had rented would need at least two hours to reach that vicinity.

Fortunately the sea was calm. The swells didn't top three feet. Bolan kept the throttle in and burned all the lights the launch carried, to warn fishermen and romantic yachtsmen of a speedboat that meant business, that wouldn't turn away from every boat that might cross its course.

Yvette showed some signs of motion sickness, but she kept her cool and tested the portable radar. It picked up half a dozen small boats ahead and two bigger vessels to starboard, but its range didn't reach nearly as far as the vicinity the *Santa Margherita* had reached by now. She called the headquarters of Police Judiciare in Nice, speaking in a code that was simple enough but put her conversation well beyond Bolan's French—and, they hoped, beyond the yacht radio operator's comprehension. At the last sighting by a police helicopter working off the Nice beaches, Muro's vessel had changed course slightly and was heading out to sea.

The launch slammed the water; the outboard roared. Yvette was miserable. She was tough, but the constant pitch and roll of the boat had brought her close to vomiting. Bolan glanced at his watch. He stood and kept his eyes on the water ahead. They passed fishing boats, small yachts. The lights of Sainte-Maxime, then of Saint-Raphaël, shone along the shore. A British naval vessel stood at sea to their starboard, painted white and lighted and flying ceremonial flags. A French patrol boat passed between them and the shore, running fast and dark, looking perhaps for boatloads of narcotics heading for the French coast. Yvette's portable radar showed the British ship, a major blip on the little screen, and the French boat, a smaller blip.

"The *Santa Margherita* will carry radar reflectors," she said, "to be a more distinct blip on ships' screens. She might be running dark by now."

He nodded. Yvette had to shout to be heard over the engine.

"What will you do when we find her?" Yvette asked. "What is your plan?"

He shrugged. "Nothing definite at this point."

At length they saw the lights of Cannes ahead, then those of Juan-les-Pins, Antibes and finally Nice. Yvette put the little screen of her radar down in front of Bolan, held up the antenna and swung it around. The sea here was filled with blips, most of them small, but more than a few large. They were ships at sea and big yachts.

"Mack," Yvette said ominously, nodding toward the radar screen. She put a long, pointed fingernail on one of the blips. "Look how fast that big one moves."

"What's the range?" Bolan asked.

"Fifty kilometers," she replied. "Look. He's moving toward *that* blip. Could that be the *Santa Margherita*?"

To the southeast, which was where the blips were coming from, the northern coast of Corsica was approximately a hundred miles off the French coast.

Maybe the *Santa Margherita* was on its way home, to the mountainous island where Vittorio Muro could hide Emily Grant as long as he wanted—or kill her if he wished, with no risk whatsoever of being brought to justice.

Bolan calculated that the blip was moving almost as fast as their outboard launch. The warrior had seen only one big boat that could move that fast: the Libyan attack boat he'd sunk off Cyprus. Khaddafi had more than one, and since he was using them to carry morphine base, it was reasonable to assume that another one was rendezvousing with the *Santa Margherita* to transfer a cargo.

But would the padrone risk taking a load of the stuff aboard his yacht? Bolan didn't think so. Hadn't Grimmaud and Yvette said the padrone didn't take that kind of risk?

So why would the two big boats be meeting—if, in fact, they were meeting? To transfer Emily to the Libyan boat? If Muro had identified her as an American agent, would he turn her over to the Libyans?

The blips continued to approach each other. Fortunately the range decreased rapidly as the outboard launch bounced over the choppy water toward the vessel. The fast blip was moving almost directly toward them, and they were closing on each other at something approaching fifty knots. In thirty minutes they would meet.

"We don't know who they are," Yvette warned.

"Anything moving that fast is something worth looking at," Bolan replied.

Yvette called PJ in Nice. Yes, the naval station at Toulon had identified a Libyan attack boat in international waters between Corsica and the Italian coast. It was twenty kilometers north of Cap Corse, heading toward San Remo. It was the same boat that often sped between Elba and Corsica, then turned west and crossed as far as the Balearics before turning south and speeding through between Sardinia and Tunisia, through the Strait of Sicily and back into Libyan coastal waters.

Colonel Khaddafi liked to show his flag everywhere in the Mediterranean. The boat was being shadowed by helicopters from a British carrier task force, as well as by French aircraft from Nice and Toulon.

"They watch him," Yvette said. She'd told Bolan that the French, British and Italians watched for meetings between this Libyan boat and fishing boats and yachts off the French and Italian coasts. "If he meets with the *Santa Margherita*, it will be the first time he's made rendezvous with a big yacht. We watch closely for such a meeting."

"Kill the lights," Bolan told her. "We'll track with the radar now."

They could see better when all their lights were dark. There was a faint crescent moon sailing along through clouds that often obscured it. The shoreline, more distant as they turned south and out to sea, glowed warmly. Red and green lights gleamed here and there on the Mediterranean waters: the running lights of marine traffic that followed the routes ships had followed across these waters for three thousand years. And here and there, in clusters, they saw the bright, greenish glare of the lights the fishermen hung over the prows of their boats to attract fish to their nets. Tomorrow's *fruits de mer* for a thousand fine restaurants were being hauled out of the sea tonight.

The launch closed on the fast blip, which was about ten kilometers away. It was abreast of the big, slower craft now, which might or might not be the *Santa Margherita*. It didn't slow, and passed within a kilometer or so of the big, slow blip. The vessel didn't turn toward it, and apparently a rendezvous at sea wasn't being effected.

Bolan let the range close to almost two kilometers before he throttled back the outboard and reduced its roar to a gurgling rumble. Now they could hear the diesels of the approaching fast boat, and they could see, faintly, the lights of the bigger, slower boat.

"Damn good thing we have the radar and know where he is," Bolan said. "Otherwise he'd run us over."

"There've been complaints of that."

The Libyan boat, if that was what it was, had been running without lights. Suddenly it seemed to burst aflame with white lights: its powerful spotlights cutting through the night. Bolan changed course to starboard; the fast boat was getting too close.

For a moment the speeding boat sounded a signal, an angry, piercing siren. It was possible that someone on the bridge had spotted the launch and was sounding a warning. The boat sped by a hundred meters to port, close enough for Bolan to identify it before the smaller boat was rolling in its wake. The warrior stood and stared. The vessel was a copy of the Libyan attack boat he had sunk with the Panzerfausts. He wished he had one or two now.

The Libyan craft ran on for another minute or so with lights blazing. Then they disappeared, and the vessel roared out of sight.

"I'd like to know what the hell that was all about," Bolan grunted. He throttled the outboard back to idling speed, then cut it entirely so they could listen.

"*Merde!*" Yvette whispered.

With the engine dead, with the roar of the twin diesels receding in the distance, they could hear that they weren't alone on the sea. Other small engines gurgled around them, one or two not more than fifty meters away. There were five or six boats in the area, all dark, all running their engines at idling speed.

"*Look out!* Damn! We hit it!"

They had slowly and quietly rammed a small yellow rubber boat bobbing on the water. Yvette was on her knees with her pistol steadied in both hands, aiming at the little boat. But there was no one in it. Bolan reached out with a boat hook and drew it alongside.

"Okay," he said. "Now we know."

It was a tiny yellow life raft loaded with wrapped packages—morphine base. The Libyan boat sped through the night off the French and Italian coasts, watched by French and Italian radar, making a big, defiant blip. But the little rubber life rafts it put overboard made no blips at all. And the little boats that gathered up those rubber rafts made none, either.

"It's leaking," Yvette said. She could hear the hiss of escaping air.

"Sure," Bolan replied. "And it's weighted. It'll float here for thirty minutes, maybe an hour, and if it's not found and unloaded, it'll sink. Nothing drifts ashore, and nothing is left to get caught in fish nets. One of the more clever ways to smuggle the stuff, I've got to admit."

"You can bet they're armed," Yvette said, peering around anxiously for the motorboats she could hear but couldn't yet see.

"We're in no great danger, I'd say. Probably every one of these boats is independent of every other. They scatter when they've finished here. They hardly see the boat that drops the stuff, and they run it ashore at a hundred different places, each one alone."

"What would stop them from stealing the stuff?" she asked. "I mean—"

"There's no other market for it ashore. That's been cornered. Anyway, they've got brains. They can imagine what would happen to them if they tried to cheat on the padrone and his terrorist allies."

"A treasure hunt," she mused, looking around, listening to the quiet motors.

Bolan pulled the rubber raft closer to examine it. "Uh-uh. Look. The life rafts are marked." He pointed to big black numbers painted on the yellow rubber and smeared across each package. "They're assigned. Each of them is trying to find his own."

"Let's set up a little problem for them," Yvette suggested, and she began throwing the packages overboard. "The one who finds his raft with nothing in it will be ready to kill, which means we better get out of here, too."

"Okay." Bolan restarted the outboard. "But I'd still like to know if that's the *Santa Margherita* over there—and if it is, what's she doing?"

"Not picking up rubber rafts, you can be damned sure."

"I'd like to get a little closer."

They found themselves weaving through a small swarm of bobbing motorboats, all of them circling, risking an occasional light, looking for the yellow rubber life rafts painted with their assigned numbers. They moved slowly, examining each raft, taking the packages or pushing the raft away and moving on. Bolan steered within a few meters of some of these boats, and the men aboard ignored him. To them he and Yvette were just another man and woman looking for their assigned raft and a quick and substantial profit.

Gunning the engine, Bolan sped toward the lighted yacht that continued moving slowly, majestically south, aloof from the activity on the water.

"I can't think it's just coincidence," Bolan said, "that the *Santa Margherita*—if that is the *Santa Margherita*—came out here and passed within half a mile of the Libyan boat. Vittorio Muro wouldn't risk being identified with the Libyan boat unless it's for a reason."

"They kept enough distance to be two distinct radar blips," Yvette reminded him, "and the Libyan passed at high speed. It wouldn't have the appearance of a rendezvous."

"The *Santa Margherita* could put out a boat to make the rendezvous," Bolan suggested.

"But we've agreed the padrone wouldn't risk taking morphine base aboard his yacht."

"It's possible the Libyan boat dropped a man," said Bolan. "They—"

Yvette lifted her shoulders in a characteristically Gallic shrug. "Speculation."

In a few minutes they were within a few hundred yards of the big, black-hulled yacht. It *was* the *Santa Margherita*—distinctive, unmistakable.

"Now you know. What are you going to do? What *can* you do?"

Yvette was right. He couldn't get close enough to board. The crew would hear and see him. He couldn't follow the yacht all night; the launch didn't carry enough fuel.

"Do you realize how important it is, what we've found out tonight? We can break up—"

Yvette shrieked as a bullet slammed into the hull of the launch, showering her with splinters. Bolan spun the launch into a fast turn, and he heard the crack of another shot. Suddenly the night was hideous with a glaring white light, a spotlight directed squarely on them. Yvette, on her knees, aimed her pistol with both hands and fired at the light. Her third shot slammed home, and the big spotlight exploded in red flame. More bullets glanced off the hull and deck of the launch.

They were outgunned. Whoever was firing at them had weapons more powerful than pistols. Yvette emptied two magazines in the direction of the incoming rounds as Bolan whipped the launch from side to side, trying to evade fire.

Suddenly Yvette was on her feet, dangerously exposed, and Bolan yelled at her to get down. At first he couldn't see what she was doing, then he realized she was pulling the pin from a grenade. She couldn't hope to reach the boat; she wouldn't be able to lob it that far. But he couldn't stop her. The warrior heard the grenade splash into the water, and after three or four seconds the water glowed dull red. They heard a muted thump and a geyser roared up from the underwater explosion.

The other boat turned away abruptly. As Yvette had guessed, the explosion scared somebody badly. Rounds continued to strafe the launch, but now the gunner had more respect. He fired from a greater distance and his shots went wild. The bullets whuffed through the air, close but not close enough.

Bolan had time to aim and fire. He braced himself and leveled the Lahti in both hands, snapping out five shots in quick succession. He hit someone; the attacking boat—a distinctive dark shadow against the gray-dark water and sky—began to turn and wallow, as if he'd hit the man at the wheel.

"Hand me a couple of those grenades. You steer," Bolan growled. "I can toss them four times as far. If I get just one into that boat—"

She handed him two grenades and spun the wheel to turn the launch toward the listing boat. Bolan wrenched out a pin and threw a grenade. It fell short, but the explosion shook the attack boat and damaged its hull. The vessel turned away once again, as if someone had taken control, replacing the man Bolan had taken out.

The warrior planted his feet wide, cocked his shoulder and threw another bomb. This time he heard the grenade land in the boat, could hear it rattle around. Someone screamed just as the grenade went off. The explosion opened a gaping hole in the hull and the boat immediately settled low in the water. Its engine stopped.

"Let's go home, lady," Bolan said. "Those were the padrone's boys, I'll bet you anything. I don't think they should get a closer look at us—that is, if any of them are left alive."

Yvette swung the launch around and headed for Saint-Tropez.

7

If, when Bolan had seen Emily in shackles on the rear deck of the *Santa Margherita*, he'd kept his binoculars trained on her a few more minutes, he would have seen a sailor kneel and unlock the leg irons. Vittorio Muro had readily accepted her explanation that she'd understood his order to be to *go* to her cabin, not necessarily to stay there. In fact, while Bolan was watching, Muro had already sent for the key, and he and Emily had been chatting amiably, even laughing about the shackles on her ankles.

Quite obviously—as she well understood, since she was still alive—no one had seen her slip over the side of the yacht and peer into the padrone's cabin while he was conferring with his visitors. She had witnessed the conference and had guessed its meaning.

After she ate breakfast with Muro, Emily returned to her cabin to shower. When she came out of the head she discovered that her white bikini and pink shirt had disappeared, and in their place on the bed lay a new bikini: small, tight and yellow, with a yellow terry-cloth jacket. Muro's girls wore what he wanted them to wear.

He didn't ask their consent to discard their clothing and substitute what he chose.

The padrone had gone ashore. There were no signs that the men she'd seen last night were still aboard. Emily returned to the lounge and joined Barbara, who was moaning that she was likely to be put ashore soon. She wore a silk jacket and nothing else, hoping that her charms would inspire Muro to keep her aboard another week. She told Emily in complete innocence that the few days she'd spent on the yacht were the best of her life. What she had paid for these days she had paid gladly and would pay again, any time.

"I'm not likely to be asked aboard another boat as nice as this one. And neither are you, don't forget. He's an easy man to please, really. Easier than some of the customers who used to come into our shop."

"You really should go home," Emily said. "You've had a great adventure. Like you said, it won't be easy to find another experience as good as this one."

"I'm not a whore, you know. I just *had* to do something in life besides work as a London shop girl."

"I understand. But take my advice and go home now, Barbara. Before you see the bad side of this kind of life."

"You've seen it, have you?"

Emily nodded. "I've seen it."

Vittorio Muro returned a little after noon and ordered lunch to be set up in the lounge. Out of the sun, he said. Barbara cast the silk jacket aside and let him look at her as he nibbled distractedly on a filet of white fish and sipped from a glass of white Bordeaux; but it did her no good; after lunch he told her she couldn't remain on the boat after three that afternoon. He gave her twenty thousand francs in cash—almost four thousand dollars for her two weeks aboard the *Santa Margherita*—and wished her good fortune.

Barbara wasn't subtle in mixing gratitude for the money with disappointment that she couldn't stay longer and earn more. She was almost tearful when she left the lounge after lunch to shove her few personal things into a duffel bag and trek unnoticed to the gangway.

The padrone used a peremptory gesture of two fingers to order Emily to drop the top part of the yellow bikini. "As to you," he said. "Have you obligations ashore? I mean, have you any that can't wait?"

"None. I'd be happy to stay aboard."

"Hmm... Well, I offer you a choice. If you choose to stay aboard after, say, four this afternoon, you will have to remain with me a week. At least a week, and maybe longer. I am taking *Santa Margherita* to sea."

"May I ask where?"

The tanned, lined face of the padrone hardened in an angry scowl for an instant. He wasn't accustomed to direct questions from his bare good-time girls. For a moment he glared at her, then he drew a breath and shrugged. "Home. I am a Corsican, you understand. I am going home for a few days."

"I've never seen Corsica," Emily replied, feigning innocent curiosity. "I've heard a lot about it and would like to see it, I think."

"It is a beautiful island," Muro said almost wistfully. "God's island. We live a very different kind of life there."

"I'd like to see it," Emily stated decisively.

"Then..." He rested his chin in his hand, deep in thought. "Maybe you could entertain my friends. Sing for them."

"I don't really sing very well, *signor*," Emily said, "or play very well. I do it to entertain myself, mostly. Also to pick up a little money. But if you think I play well enough to entertain your friends, I will. Well, at least I'll do my very best."

"We will hold the question in reserve," Muro decided. "But if you wish to come to Corsica, I promise you, Linda, a short visit to a place you will not soon forget."

THE HELMSMAN TURNED southeast, and the big yacht cruised slowly along the Riviera coast. The padrone appeared on the rear deck in shorts, and stretched out in a chair to sun himself. He wore dark glasses, which he took off from time to time so he could press a pair of large binoculars to his eyes. He sipped a refreshing glass of white-wine sangría and encouraged Emily to drink it, too. She'd come aboard with nothing but her white bikini and pink shirt—which had been laundered and had reappeared in her cabin—and her guitar case and the explosives it contained. She had nothing else to wear but what he provided: this afternoon a floppy straw beach hat to protect her head from the sun, a lace jacket that afforded some protection to her shoulders and the bottom half of still another bikini, this one blue. Emily sat facing Muro, in a comfortable deck chair, with her guitar across her lap, strumming experimentally and softly. Muro enjoyed her quiet music and seemed at times to doze behind his sunglasses.

"Tonight," he said abruptly, "I will once again require you to confine yourself to your cabin for an hour or two. For reasons of my own that I cannot discuss with you, I will be compelled to impose some restraint on you. Only for a short time, though. You suffered no pain last night, you said—only a little discomfort. You do not, I believe, take offense, do you, Linda?"

"No, *signor*," she said quietly. This was interesting, perhaps important. What could he have in mind? If she was correct in her assumption that the men she'd seen last night weren't still on board, then...

"Not overnight," he said. "I was annoyed with you last night and thought to teach you a lesson by leaving your leg irons on until this morning. Tonight..." He shrugged. "Only for a few hours."

"I'm from Texas, *signor*," she replied. "I don't know anything about the way Europeans do business. Even so, I'm smart enough not to ask you why it's so important that I not see anything." She smiled. "I'm curious, but I'm not stupid enough to pursue my curiosity."

"Yes. If I didn't suppose you are that intelligent, I wouldn't have you aboard."

AFTER DINNER Muro accompanied Emily to her cabin. This time he chained her himself, making a great point of being gentle and apologetic, but locking the leg irons in place as they had been previously and adding to them a length of chain secured to the bed springs by two padlocks. The chain was long enough for her to hobble to any point in her cabin, including the head. He promised Emily he'd return within the hour to free her; and, so saying, he went out and doubly assured himself of her confinement by locking her door.

What could she do but lie on her bed and wait to be unchained? The cabin was equipped with a television set, and she flipped across the channels, looking for something distracting, finding nothing. There were books on a shelf above the bed, in French, Italian and Spanish, but nothing in English. She chose an Italian translation of a John Updike novel and lay back on the bunk to read.

She heard the roaring speed boat long before she could make out even its shadow as she gazed through her cabin porthole. Its shadow, when she saw it, was ominous—a sleek gray shape bearing down on the *Santa Margherita* at great speed. She wondered if it could be a French or Italian patrol boat, and if so, might it fire on the yacht? If the yacht sank, she'd drown; she couldn't escape the chains. With an eerie sense of mystery and dread, she watched the big boat approach. At what seemed like the last possible moment, it slowed for a moment, then suddenly veered away and picked up speed. A minute or two later it blazed with light and sounded a shrieking siren. It ran lighted for a short time, then went dark again, and the roar of its engines gradually faded as it sped away.

It was a mysterious episode, a rendezvous at sea and yet not a rendezvous. And afterward, she could hear the small, buzzing engines of little boats in the vicinity.

Odd. Emily sat down on the bunk and examined her leg irons. Being manacled or shackled was something she hadn't expected when she elected to pursue her personal cause, yet it had happened to her once before, and now she found herself locked in heavy and secure fetters. They weren't the same as the ones she'd worn last night, and she concluded it would be more than difficult to escape from them—even if escape was a good idea. Escape was in fact impossible, except maybe if she could work on the locks. She—

Shots! Small-arms fire cracked across the water. Whatever had transpired, it had been done smoothly, but now something was wrong. She felt the big engines of the yacht turn up to higher revolutions, and the *Santa Margherita* began to pick up speed, as if preparing to flee from some threat on the water.

The gunfire persisted. She heard the grunt of an underwater explosion, then another. Then she saw a flash and heard the bark of a surface explosion. Someone was firing heavy stuff.

Oddly, the explosions remained at a distance from the yacht, which didn't appear to be the target. And then . . . silence. She heard another buzzing small engine, pulling away and fading. Then the sea fell silent, and the engines of the *Santa Margherita* slowed again, to their normal speed. The incident was over.

When the man arrived to unlock her shackles, she was reading again. "Signor Muro," he told her, "wishes you to come immediately to his suite."

She rubbed her ankles for a moment, picked up her guitar case and walked out of the cabin. She walked unattended to the grand, luxurious master suite, where she'd spent the past two nights.

Vittorio Muro sat slumped in a lounge chair, with a glass of red wine in his hand, looking glumly out at the dark sea where now only an occasional dim light glowed in the distance. Emily put her guitar case aside and poured a glass of wine for herself.

For a minute or two he seemed to ignore her. Then he spoke. "Play and sing for me, Linda. Play the songs I heard you playing on the quay the other morning. Later, I will ask you for more energetic entertainment, but now I would like my spirits lifted."

"I heard the shots and explosions. I'm not such a fool as to ask what happened, but was it bad for you, *signor*?"

"I lost a business associate," Muro admitted. "Assassinated. He was to have come aboard, dropped from another boat and picked up by a launch from the *Santa Margherita*. Our launch was attacked. We've been able to pick up one wounded man only. Three other members of my crew and my business associate were shot, or killed in the explosions, or drowned."

"I'm sorry, *signor*."

"I am a businessman, Linda. Surely you understand that when a man enjoys success, others envy him—

others hate him, in fact. This has happened before. There are those who would like to murder me."

"That song you sang on the quay," he continued, tossing back his wine. "'Memory.' Sing it for me, Linda."

"I don't do it well," she said. "It's too much for my vocal range. But—"

"Even so, it sounded good to me."

She sang.

BEFORE DAWN, *Santa Margherita* put in at the port of Bastia, Corsica, and after a quick breakfast the padrone took Emily, who was dressed now in a long black skirt and a white blouse, in a Mercedes limousine on the road for his villa in the Corsican mountains. She sat with him in the rear seat. A chauffeur drove, and an ominous-looking man in a black suit sat in the front seat beside him. Emily wasn't able to figure out the direction they took, over what roads they traveled, or even how far they went. She could see only that they drove on ever-deteriorating roads, higher into the mountains, into remote countryside, wooded and rugged.

She knew when the limousine left the public highway and drove onto a private road; the private road was better maintained, its drainage ditches in good repair so that the summer rains had not rutted the roadbed, and a thick coat of coarse, loose gravel crunched under the tires. The road climbed steeply up a mountain, often reversing in hairpin turns, and always in the shadow of thick forest. Once she caught sight of a man with a big gun standing on the bank above the road. He didn't look like a hunter; more likely he was a sentinel.

They were on the private road for what seemed like a long time, and eventually the woods thinned. They emerged onto a broad mountain meadow where sheep grazed. The view was breathtaking. To the right as the Mercedes continued upward she could see the Mediterranean, gleaming with blinding brightness in the early-morning sun. To the left she could peer up at the summit of the mountain, still a thousand feet or more above them. Then ahead . . . the villa. A vision.

It was a rambling building, or, rather, group of buildings. Some of it was of old gray stone and had been built, she guessed, by the Normans more than seven hundred years ago. Part of it had once stood behind walls; the crumbled ruin of a high stone wall extended along the seaward side. A church, also of the old gray stone, stood at the center, its modest square tower surmounted by a wrought-iron cross.

What appeared to be the main building of the villa was of far more recent construction: a stark white-stucco house with the red tile roof so characteristic of the nearby Italian Riviera. It was less than a century old, she judged. Still other buildings in the jumbled complex represented various centuries between the medieval century when the church was built and the nineteenth when the house went up.

Scores of people lived there: the padrone's family and retainers. As the limousine passed through a wide, rough gap in the old stone wall, men at the roadside doffed their caps and bowed. The approach of the limousine had been noted in the villa, and as it pulled to a stop in the courtyard, in front of the entrance to the main house, half a dozen people scurried out to stand on the steps and offer greeting. It was a scene from the eighteenth century, Emily mused. If only they had arrived in a coach and the servants at the door wore powdered wigs.

Muro ordered her to stay in the car; she'd be taken care of shortly. He stepped out majestically and calmly received homage, like a medieval lord being greeted by his vassals.

The chauffeur drove on, pulling the car into the shelter of a small outbuilding, what would have been a carport in a more modern setting. The man she'd guessed was a bodyguard opened the door beside her and beckoned her out. *"Per piacere,"* he growled, indicating that she should go where he pointed. He led her, without another word, through a back door of the main house, up a flight of narrow back stairs and into a handsome broad corridor. He opened a heavy, dark-wood door—she noticed it was equipped with a heavy bolt on the outside—and admitted her to what was apparently to be her room during her stay in the villa.

It was a lovely room, with a small balcony and a magnificent view of the mountainside and the Mediterranean. The dark, wide planking of the floor contrasted with gleaming white walls. Lush green plants grew in big clay pots on both sides of the window and on the balcony. The furnishings included a wide brass bed, a bureau with mirror, even a television set and a radio. A tiled bath contained towels, soap, shampoo, bath oil, perfume. It was as though she had a room in a five-star hotel. Except for one thing. Her door was bolted from the outside.

Nobody could possibly know where she was. Emily was on her own.

8

Bolan had raced for shore, trying to catch up with one of the boats that had taken morphine base from a yellow rubber life raft, but he'd been delayed too long by the fight with the launch from the *Santa Margherita,* and the boats had scattered in the dark. Yvette had radioed the Police Judiciare in Nice, and patrol boats went out to attempt intercepts. Unfortunately hundreds of fishing boats and other small craft were coming ashore in the early-morning hours, and not a single package of base was found. The captain of one patrol boat suspected packages had been thrown overboard as he approached, but that was the closest anyone came to an interception.

The rental agent at Saint-Tropez had understood his launch had been rented by police agents, so he raised no questions about the bullet holes and only remarked dryly that he assumed PJ would take care of the damage. Yvette assured him that all damage would be fully paid for.

Bolan and Yvette returned to his room at the Byblos about the time the sun rose through another of the morning mists that were typical of the Riviera at that time of year, and they were able to get about three hours' sleep before it was time for her to get up and go to work. Both were exhausted.

As Yvette sat at the foot of the bed applying with elaborate care the dramatic makeup she wore as a fashion model, she stared thoughtfully at Bolan. He was a handsome man, in his own mature, rugged way. Not every woman would have found him so; it took a perceptive woman to see how very handsome he was. He lay on the bed they shared, wearing nothing but a pair of briefs. His lean body was well-muscled and bore many scars. He seemed the very image of self-confidence, strength personified. You could count on Mack Bolan. And Yvette knew she'd want him fighting in her corner.

She couldn't fall in love with him, she knew that already. God forbid. The woman who did would enter a living hell, not of his making, but of the life to which he was committed and couldn't abandon. Yvette had no illusion that he would ever give up the ideal to which he was so deeply committed.

So what of Emily Grant?

"Have you ever let yourself fall in love, Monsieur Bolan? Emily is so attractive."

Bolan shrugged. "You don't 'let yourself.' You just do it, if it happens."

"Still . . ."

"It doesn't make any difference," he said firmly. "Love? I don't know. All I know is that I've got a damn competent colleague who's in big trouble. One way or the other, I've got to do something about Emily."

"Understood," Yvette said.

"The question is, do we attack from here or go to Corsica? If we can make trouble for him here, Muro will return."

"You can't go to Corsica," Yvette warned. "He's on his own ground there and has every advantage."

"He's got Emily, that's his big advantage. I can't just sit here."

"Maybe it's not his big advantage. Maybe he still doesn't know who she is. In fact, you can be sure he doesn't if she's still alive. But if somebody shows up in Corsica looking for her, then he'll understand."

"So what do you suggest?"

"Be patient. Keep on working from here. The key to Emily's safety in Corsica might lie in what you can do here."

Bolan nodded. He swung his legs over the side of the bed, walked to the window and looked down at the swimming pool, where three bare-breasted girls lounged in the morning sun. He wondered if they were as carefree as they looked or if they had problems to solve like everyone else.

"A lot of morphine base came ashore last night," he said. "Right now, while we're sitting here gabbing, it's on the way to the lab. No wonder there was no unusual traffic yesterday. The shipment arrived last night. It's being delivered this morning."

"We can sit here and 'gab,' as you put it, all we want," she replied. "Police Judiciare is out looking for that traffic. We have roadblocks in place. Cars and trucks are being stopped. A hundred uniformed policemen are working on this and nothing else all day, as well as a dozen plainclothes agents. Good men, too. I don't think we could contribute much to the process."

"So you're going to model some clothes today."

"Yes, to keep my cover intact. And what are you going to do to keep yours intact?"

"What would you suggest I do?" he asked impatiently. "Go to the beach?"

"You could do worse. If you have nothing more productive to do, then do something to make your cover more believable."

MACK BOLAN DROVE to Plage de Tahiti, the miles-long beach just outside of the town, where on a summer day tens of thousands of sun worshipers jostled for space on the sand and in the cool Mediterranean water. As a registered guest at the Byblos Hotel Bolan was entitled to rent a lounge chair. He settled back on one with a pitcher of sangría at his side, and scanned the boats off the beach through his binoculars.

Speedboats raced by, threading their way among anchored yachts of all sizes. He didn't try to count the yachts, but a rough estimate would put the number at fifty, with two or three magnificent big ones. There were scores of small craft, and every yacht and boat, it seemed, had its quota of nudes. On the beach, the girls were topless. On the boats, people were stark naked, men and women alike. A few of them swam in the water around their boats, but most lounged on the decks, eating, drinking, yelling, laughing.

The traffic along this stretch of water was constant and heavy. It was easy to see why the French had an impossible task. Any one of the vessels that seemed to be delivering food and drink to the yachts could actually be delivering drugs.

Bolan watched one boat after another, the powerful binoculars almost taking him aboard. He studied the faces of the men and women lounging naked on the decks. It seemed unlikely that any of the giggling, drunken revelers could be involved in the grim trade in heroin. On this assumption, he concentrated his attention on the yachts where the people were dressed and looked a little more businesslike.

One yacht in particular held his attention. There were four men aboard and one blond girl—the men wearing shorts and shirts, the girl conventionally dressed for this place, in a bikini bottom only. The men seemed engaged in earnest conversation, and one of them scanned the sea horizon with powerful binoculars. Whoever they were, whatever they were doing, they weren't enjoying the sunny waters off Saint-Tropez with the same enthusiasm of the other pleasure seekers. Their talk seemed angry at times. One man made conversational points with stabbing gestures, fingers into palm.

As the wind shifted and swung the yacht around, Bolan's eye was caught by something more interesting. Lying on the foredeck was a yellow object. A yellow rubber life raft? Perhaps. There was nothing unusual about that. He'd noticed several others. They were used to paddle ashore, to splash in the surf, to pick up wine and beer to take back out to the yachts, to drop off people who were leaving the boats. There were other yellow rubber boats bobbing on the waves. But this one...

This one was deflated—a deflated yellow rubber life raft, lying on the foredeck of that boat where men with their clothes on were engaged in earnest, even angry, conversation.

It was worth investigating.

When the yacht swung around in the wind Bolan read the lettering on the stern: the *Mistral*, and its home port was Antibes.

INSPECTOR MAURICE GRIMMAUD nodded. "Yes," he said. "A yacht called *Mistral* is registered at Antibes. The owner is a Monsieur Robert Thuret, a man of means, but he is not immensely wealthy. The boat is his plaything. The blond girl you saw aboard is probably his daughter, Brigitte. She is nineteen and quite beautiful. Monsieur Thuret is in the business of manufacturing—you will find this difficult to believe—ligatures. I mean, you understand, the thread surgeons use to sew us up after they have cut an incision in us."

"His sales representatives," Bolan guessed, "undoubtedly travel over the entire continent, selling his product to doctors and hospitals."

"Precisely," Grimmaud said with a grin.

"And they cross international frontiers at will and without much question."

"To be sure."

"And, perhaps, carry—"

"Heroin? No, I think not." A Gallic shrug. "Well…
Maybe. It could be."

"Where is the *Mistral* now?" Bolan asked.

Another shrug. "Uh, still lying off Plage de Tahiti, I
believe."

"How do I get aboard?"

"Oh, I think you don't, *monsieur*."

Bolan shot him a piercing look. "Six or seven boats
came ashore last night, carrying a load of pain and
death. Together we didn't succeed in stopping a single
kilo. We don't know where it went to be refined into
heroin. This is the only lead we've got, Grimmaud. I
intend to check it out."

"We could have the navy board the boat, I suppose," Grimmaud suggested.

"And find nothing," Bolan snapped impatiently.
"They wouldn't be fool enough to have it aboard. It's
gone, Grimmaud, and on its way to the streets. And you
know what it'll do there. Anyway, even if we find some
of it, then what? I sank a hundred kilos of it, probably
more, off Cyprus. Yvette threw a few kilos into the water last night. And those are losses they can afford to
take. I want the lab, Grimmaud. Then I want the padrone."

Grimmaud raised his eyebrows. "You have a certain…ability to do what others can't." He shrugged.
"Do as you see fit."

Bolan smiled grimly. "And if I screw up, you'll swear
you never heard of me."

Grimmaud smiled. "Of course. If I—how is the American idiom?—'screwed up,' wouldn't you deny you'd ever heard of me?"

BOLAN RETURNED to the beach just before sunset. Most of the boats were gone. Only one of the big yachts remained at anchor. The *Mistral* was gone. Back to Antibes? No. Fortunately—though it took him a little while to find it—the yacht had only circled the point, as many other vessels had done, and returned to Saint-Tropez. That was their daily routine: out to the water off the beach during the day, back to the town at night. The *Mistral* wasn't big enough—or maybe its owner wasn't rich enough—to claim a spot backed to the quay; it was tied up at a slip in the new yacht basin.

It was easy enough to stroll through the marina and look at the boats. He walked up to the *Mistral* and stood looking at it, like any curious American or English tourist. As compared to anything but the *Santa Margherita* and the other multimillion-dollar boats, this one was expensive and enviably comfortable.

The blonde—Thuret's daughter, if Grimmaud was correct in his identification—was on the rear deck, sitting at a table, sipping white wine. She was modestly dressed now, in both pieces of her little black bikini, which was covered by a loose black silk jacket. She cast a quick, casual glance at Bolan, followed by a more interested, lingering glance. She lifted her chin and smiled at him.

Bolan returned her smile but didn't speak. Instead, he strolled past, pretending disinterest. Too much curiosity might be noticed by one of the men on board. He would return later for a closer look.

He left the hotel after midnight, leaving Yvette asleep in his room. Once in his car, he changed into a pair of camouflage fatigues and smeared his face with dull green combat cosmetics. He would rather have had his black nightsuit with all its equipment, but that was something else he'd been compelled to let sink with the rubber boat. The fatigues had been purchased in a waterfront shop in Saint-Tropez.

The warrior parked the car along the roadside just west of town and made his way over sandy soil and through coarse salt grass toward the rocks and gravel at the edge of the water. The area he'd chosen wasn't fine sandy beach; this was rough coastline, like most of the Riviera waterfront.

Saint-Tropez in summer is choked with tourists. The young and impecunious camp everywhere, sleeping in small tents, some simply putting their sleeping bags down in ditches along the roads. Some were out here, many of whom were awake, drinking wine and laughing, by the light of small lanterns. It would have been easy to stumble over one of them, and the Executioner wondered what sort of alarm would be sounded if anyone saw an armed man with green smeared across his face. Fortunately the only people he nearly tripped over were coupling and were so intent on their efforts that they didn't bother even to look up.

Bolan reached the edge of the water, slipped in and swam out a few yards. The fatigues were light—more Saint-Tropez stylish than practical—and didn't impede his swimming. He began a slow, easy swim, back toward the town. When he was passing dark villas, where the sleeping-bag tourists would be closed off the property, he swam ashore and walked along the edge of the water. Alternately swimming and walking, he reached the town again in less than an hour.

Bolan didn't risk climbing over the breakwater and entering the new yacht basin by the most direct route. Instead, he swam around and entered the Saint-Tropez basins through the main entry, under the winking lighthouse on the bigger breakwater known as the Môle.

Now, with only his head above water, taking gentle, quiet breaststrokes, he entered the new basin and made his way toward the *Mistral*.

People were still awake on some of the yachts, sitting out in the starlit night, their conversation, cigar and cigarette smoke drifting across the water.

The *Mistral*, when he reached it, was one of those boats whose occupants were still awake. But not on deck. Curtains covered the windows of the cabin, but Bolan could see that the main cabin was brightly lighted. He swam to the stern, took a grip on the rudder and waited there in the water for a time, surveying the area, listening.

Fortunately the nearest boats were dark and silent.

The *Mistral*, like most of the smaller yachts, had a swimming platform attached to the stern and a ladder that led to the deck. Bolan heaved himself onto the platform, knelt there for two or three minutes to let the water drip from his fatigues, so it wouldn't splash on the deck when he climbed aboard. Then he made his way up the ladder between the platform and the deck.

Bolan crouched on the rear deck, alert to any sound. He felt certain no one was topside on the yacht, but he needed to be sure that no one on the dock or on another boat had seen him leave the platform. After a minute or so, he began to work his way silently forward, intent on examining the deflated raft he'd spotted on the foredeck.

His suspicions were confirmed: the yellow rubber boat, marked with an identification number, was exactly what he'd seen last night floating in the Mediterranean. The logical conclusion was that the *Mistral* had been at sea last night and had brought in a consignment of morphine base. That made things easier. If the probe went hard, he'd be hitting the right people.

Bolan crawled on knees and elbows across the foredeck to the front windows of the main cabin and chanced a quick look. But he could see nothing through the heavy draperies. Scanning the area again to make sure no one was watching, he climbed the cabin and made his way across its roof toward the rear. From there he could enter the topside bridge where he could gaze down into the forward part of the main cabin, through the hatch that connected the cabin with the bridge.

Bolan flattened himself on the deck and peered down into the warmly lighted, wood-paneled cabin. Cigar smoke floated up through the hatch. So did conversation, in three male voices and one female—Thuret's daughter he supposed.

They spoke a French dialect, fast and idiomatic. He could follow the basic conversation, but he missed a lot. The gist of it concerned Emily, who was said to be a *"flic Americain,"* working with a male agent. He was encouraged by understanding them to say her face was unknown, as was his own. Then one said there had been a tall, dark-haired woman in the launch that had tried to interfere with the previous night's delivery. The woman with the agent, they assumed, was Emily Grant. Someone had gotten a glimpse of Bolan's face but didn't see enough to describe him. And that same someone had mistaken Yvette for Emily.

The female voice used the title "il padrone" more than the others did. The woman seemed to dominate the conversation, and she spoke very rapidly in French that bore the heavy accent of some other language. Her voice was so harsh that Bolan couldn't believe it was the voice of the daughter, the pretty blonde he'd seen on the rear deck of the *Mistral*.

Suddenly a door slammed below, and Bolan watched as a man sauntered onto the deck. The Executioner made him instantly. They were all alike, these types, wherever you found them. The guy was an enforcer, no doubt bored with the conversation inside, and had come on deck for a smoke and to survey the night. The hard bulge in his right pocket had the unmistakable shape of a small automatic.

Bolan crouched and watched the enforcer walk along the deck, smoking the way Europeans do: holding the cigarette between thumb and finger instead of between two fingers in the American style. The enforcer ambled back to the stern. If the man had been observant he would have noticed the water on the deck—water that had dripped off Bolan's fatigues.

The man turned and walked slowly back toward the cabin. When Bolan had his first full view of the gunner's face, he narrowed his eyes in concentration. He knew the guy—Anthony "Deacon" Dicomano. Bolan had first encountered him in Miami years ago, again in Palermo in the recent past. The man was deadly, cruel and, as it had proved, elusive. It was Dicomano who had murdered Julia Empoli. Bolan was sure of it, though Dicomano wasn't wanted for that killing. The Casciano Family had wanted his balls for that one, but they hadn't dared to touch him. If he was with Muro, that would explain their hands-off policy. Not one Family in the States would dare cross the Union Corse.

Dicomano didn't climb to the bridge. He began to thread his way along the narrow walkway between the rail and the main cabin. As he sauntered past Bolan's position, the warrior leaned over and struck him hard on the head with the butt of the Lahti automatic. The enforcer sagged against the cabin wall, clawing at his pocket for his own weapon. Bolan's grip tightened around his throat.

"Old score settled, Deacon," he muttered as Dicomano thrashed in his grip. Bolan snapped the gunner's head back and broke his neck.

He left the limp body lying on the deck and slipped over the railing and into the water. They'd come up and find him after a while. The corpse was bound to raise a lot of questions.

9

A sour-faced woman entered Emily's room bearing clothing and jewelry: a skirt of black embroidery with colored threads in patterns of flowers and leaves, and a white lace blouse; a heavy gold necklace and a bracelet of gold chain. But still no shoes; she was to remain barefoot. The woman spoke to her in Italian and told her to dress in what she had brought her. Il Grande, which was what she called Muro, wanted song and the music of her guitar with his lunch.

"Be sure you're clean before you put those clothes on," the woman ordered scornfully before she left the room and once more bolted the door. "They've been worn by better women than you." Her final word to Emily, spat back through the door as it banged shut, was *sudiciona*, which meant "harlot."

The woman returned a few minutes later to let her out of the room and sullenly lead her to a broad stone terrace overlooking the shoreline. She scowled angrily when Muro nodded toward a chair and quietly told Emily to be seated and to pour herself a glass of wine.

"This is my home," he said proudly. "My family has lived here for more than three hundred years. Before that . . . well, others. The property was once a monastery. Then the home of my ancestors. Each generation has added to it. You will forgive my pride."

"Pride isn't something that needs to be forgiven, *signor*."

"It is very old pride," he said with a smile. "A tradition in my family."

"Your family owned this before the French came, then?"

"Yes. Before the invaders, the usurpers came. Corsica has a proud history, Linda, and my family has played its part. My ancestor who took this property found it in ruins, the ruins of a monastery whose lazy, worldly monks had long since abandoned it. He rebuilt the church first, because he was an intensely religious man. Each of my ancestors had added to his work. This terrace is my work. I like to believe my son and his son and generations after them will sit here and view the mountains and the sea. I pray in a chapel restored by my remote ancestor. I read in a library collected by my great-grandfather, my grandfather and my father. I find comfort, not only in prayer and study and in sitting here, contemplating the grandeur of the world, but also in contemplating the long continuity of this place and all that we have here. I want to think that continuity will endure for generations after me."

Emily concealed her sense of irony in this talk of prayer, study and continuity, from a man whose life work was murder.

"Your home is beautiful. The buildings, the mountains, the forest. We don't have mountains like this in Texas."

"But others," he said, "with desert and rocks, like North Africa, no? Wild and beautiful in a different way. I have seen pictures. I have always wanted to go there."

"I hope you come to Texas," she said. "I hope you will visit me and my family."

He laughed. "That would scandalize your town and family. A visit from Vittorio Muro, the padrone from Corsica. Your newspapers would tell scandalous stories about me, as European newspapers do."

"You must be a very successful man, Signor Muro, to own so elegant an estate."

"I have many business interests," he admitted. "When you have many, some are bound to be profitable."

They ate a simple lunch. Emily played and sang for him. She wasn't really a musician—she played the guitar only for quiet fun. Anything very complex was beyond her ability, and she was compelled to tell him she couldn't play any of the operatic arias he suggested he would like to hear.

"This afternoon," he told her, "I am expecting the arrival of several business associates, and I will assemble them for a meeting immediately after dinner. I would like you to dine with us, and I will send appropriate clothes for the occasion. It pleases me to show them how many attractive young women I can bring to my yacht and villa. After dinner, however, I will have to send you to your room. I must ask you not to be distressed if your door is locked."

"No chains, *signor*?" she asked with a smile.

He returned her smile. "No chains. I regret having to do that to you, Linda, but aboard the *Santa Margherita* things are not so secure. This evening, anyway, will be a very private business conference, and one I think you would find most boring. Afterward, I will come to your room. You need not try to stay awake for me. I am likely to be very late. My business associates are windy men, and not all of them speak the same languages. All their flowery rhetoric has to be translated."

"You won't ask me to sing and play for your guests, I hope."

"I will ask you to sing for me later," he replied. "Anticipation of that will relieve my boredom during a long business meeting." He smiled. "I will be talking hard business and thinking of the soft pink flesh I will be privileged to touch later."

Emily laughed, feigning delight. He wasn't, in fact, a terribly demanding man, and was easily satisfied. She didn't feel profaned by her contact with him.

"This afternoon," he continued, "I will have someone show you around the villa. I have given instructions that your door is not to be locked until after dinner. You are at liberty to wander about the estate as you wish. Let me warn you not to go too far from the buildings. I do have security men in the mountain woods, and they would not know who you are. Unfortunately they have been trained to treat unknown visitors very roughly. Corsican mountain men, you know. They have a certain spirit all their own.''

THE TACITURN BODYGUARD who had been with them on the drive up from Bastia and who had taken her to her room was now her guide to the villa. His name was Gaillac, and he provided a running commentary as he showed her the centuries-old stone buildings that were the core of the villa.

The chapel was the most interesting. It was small and quite spare, without stained glass or gold candlesticks or images of the saints. But it was old, and the worn old stones exuded an odor of antiquity. Masses weren't celebrated here anymore, Gaillac explained, though they'd been said in the days of the *signor*'s grandfather. The bodies of the *signor*'s ancestors were in a crypt below the altar. When Emily expressed an interest, he led her down, where, to her surprise, he pointed out a score of heavy old oaken coffins, all sitting on stone platforms and ledges, unburied.

"The padrone will rest here, at the end," Gaillac told her in a hushed voice.

Emily walked among the coffins, looking at the names on the brass plates, which were all male, the successive padrones who had ruled here.

"Where are the women?" she asked. "These men's wives?"

"Buried outside," he replied. "Only the heads of the family are here."

Another of the old buildings contained a baronial hall with an immense fireplace. The furniture had long since been removed but Gaillac explained the room had once been the monks' dining hall, and later it had become the baronial hall and council chamber for the *signor*'s ancestors. An immense carved, painted and gilded coat of arms hung above the fireplace. The motto was *Muro del Regno*—The Wall of the Kingdom.

"He himself has held meetings here," Gaillac said. "He has great tables set up, and great old chairs, and lights the room with candles." The bodyguard grinned. "That is when he wants to impress foreign visitors who have not yet learned to appreciate his tradition. Tradition is an important part of the padrone's life."

An element of the padrone's tradition, she noticed, was to be attended by armed men. Gaillac carried a pistol in a shoulder holster. Others about the estate wore big, long-barreled revolvers openly on their hips.

In the light and airy nineteenth-century building, one of the big rooms housed a floor-to-ceiling library, ten thousand volumes at least, most of them in Italian, many though in French and English. The *signor*, Gaillac remarked, treasured his books, though it was his father who had collected most of them and had spent many hours in this room, reading. The old padrone had died in that great leather chair.

When Gaillac took her back to her room, he didn't lock her in, as Muro had promised. On the pretense of returning to the library, she spent some time wandering through the halls, learning the layout of the house and where the least obvious exits were. She had no illusions that she could escape down the mountain, but it was second nature with her to orient herself. Emily returned to her room late in the afternoon and tested a little trick on the door bolt, something that might prove useful later. Then she took a nap. A long night seemed likely.

THE OLD WOMAN with the sour face bustled into the room, this time bearing another armload of clothes, what Emily was to wear to dinner. Those clothes reflected apparently what Vittorio Muro considered a vision of youth and style.

His vision was from another decade. Emily dressed in what he had sent—black velvet toreador pants and a sequined white evening sweater. She forced her feet into black spike-heeled patent-leather shoes, wondering who had worn these clothes previously. Whoever it was had been smaller than she was, and the pants and sweater fit skin tight.

The woman returned to escort Emily to dinner in the baronial hall.

The men were already seated when Emily was escorted into the room, and only Muro and the European rose from their places. The others simply stared and seemed to resent the intrusion of a young woman into their company. She took the chair Muro offered her—beside himself—and he poured her a glass of dark red wine. Glancing around the big dining room, she saw Gaillac and two other bodyguards, standing with their backs to the wall.

Emily felt awkward, but the way she looked obviously pleased the padrone. He beamed as he presented her to his guests as "Linda, my new friend from Texas. A charming girl, don't you think, gentlemen?"

He didn't tell her the names of his associates. There were four of them: one European—perhaps French, perhaps Italian—and three darker-skinned men, possibly Iranians or Libyans. All were dressed in heavy, overstyled double-breasted suits. The Arabs had mustaches and yellowish, sullen eyes that settled on Emily with unfriendly curiosity.

It became apparent to her as she sipped the rich wine and began to eat the food that was immediately placed on the table that her presence effectively stopped conversation. Muro had imposed her on the Middle Easterners, and they were impatient. The presence of a woman at the men's table offended them.

It was apparent, too, that the padrone didn't care whether they liked it or not; she was a pawn in a tactical confrontation, but Muro was in a position to play her, and they were in no position to object. They were guests in his house, on his island, and they had no choice but to glower and keep their peace.

They didn't like the dinner conversation, either. Muro chatted with Emily and the European about political developments around the world, about art, music, food and wine. He was rather well informed, she thought, on all these subjects. The swarthy trio ate quietly, listening, not participating. Their speculative glances toward her, which grew more frequent and lingering as dinner went on, were crudely carnal. She shuddered to think what might happen if she fell into their hands.

They didn't linger over the dinner. The food was good—veal and pasta in a subtle white sauce, followed by a dessert of fruits in a clear, brandy-based sauce, with soft white cheese and coffee—but a little more than an hour after it was served, the meal was finished. Muro suggested to Emily that she return to her room, that he would join her later, and she was led there by Gaillac, who this time bolted her door.

WHAT SHE WAS DOING was dangerous. But it could all be for nothing if she didn't take the risk of trying now to escape her locked room and returning to the dining room to overhear as much as she could.

She had studied every corridor, every stairway of the house during her tour with Gaillac and during her walks to and from the dining room. She had studied the wall below her little balcony. A guitar-strumming young refugee from Dallas was effectively confined by the drop from her balcony to the ground. A trained agent from Fox Den was not.

Emily kicked off the spike-heeled shoes, which would be nothing but an impediment, stripped herself of the white sweater, since it would almost glow in the starlight, and put on the top of the yellow bikini. She opened the guitar case and carefully extracted one of the thin, razor-sharp blades from the lining. She stuck that into the waistband of the toreador pants. Also in the lining of the case was a length of thin nylon cord. Emily had already cut off a couple of feet, and she pushed the short piece into one of the halves of the bikini bra. She wasn't armed as she might have wished, but these simple weapons were supplemented by training and experience.

She switched off all the lights in her bedroom and left only a dim light burning in the bathroom, as though she were sleeping while she waited for her lord and master to favor her with his presence. She was ready.

From the balcony it was easy to see that the house was guarded. The points of orange fire on the cigarettes of half a dozen guards signaled their presence as much as if they had worn neon signs. She stood for a long moment on the balcony, studying the scene, trying to see if anyone was looking toward her window. If anyone was, she couldn't see him. With practiced, athletic agility, Emily lifted herself over the century-old wrought-iron rail and lowered herself until she hung from the balcony.

Emily waited a moment, listening. Then she let go and dropped to the cobblestones below, landing painfully on her bare feet. She was in the courtyard fronting the house. She slipped away to the north and rounded the house to its north side, where she opened the window she'd unlatched during her second visit that afternoon. After a quick glance around, Emily climbed into the dark library. She'd learned earlier that Muro hadn't installed electric alarms.

The library was shrouded in darkness. She fumbled her way past the antique furniture to where she remembered the main door opened onto the corridor. Easing the door open, she checked the corridor. It was deserted. Muro relied on his outside sentries. She watched the corridor for a minute or two, but no one passed by.

She slipped out of the library, closing the door after her, and walked quickly along the long, wide, dimly lighted hall to the wing of the house where the padrone and his associates still sat—she hoped—at the dining table.

Emily had studied the room carefully during dinner. There was just one place, she judged, where she could eavesdrop: the pantry at the end of the dining room. It was there that the food was exchanged between the kitchen personnel and the butler and maid, there that the final examination was made to see that each dish was arranged as the padrone required, and that silver and glasses were shelved, ready to be given a final touch of the polishing cloth and hurried to the table as required. If her guess was right, the maid and butler would be banished from the pantry when serious business conversation began. They were no more to be trusted than she was with the secrets to be discussed that night.

Emily knew where the door was that opened into the pantry from a corridor, and not from the kitchen, which very likely was still a busy place. The door was unlocked. She opened it a crack, checked, then slipped in and crawled across the dusty floor of the pantry.

She had a view, and was within earshot of the dinner table. The men were talking earnestly, some of them irritably. And because of the necessity for translations, the conversation hadn't progressed far. The amenities were over. They were talking hard business.

"Every kilo, almost every kilo, was recovered and delivered," one of the Middle Easterners said in Italian. The European then translated into French for the benefit of the other two Middle Easterners. "The boats picked up as many rafts as they would have if nobody had tried to interfere."

"But at what cost?" asked another. He went on to complain that the secret of the little yellow rafts had been compromised. They couldn't use that method again.

"Gentlemen," Muro said calmly, "did anyone ever suggest this business would be easy, without its problems? No. I don't think so. I see no reason for anyone to be excited. So far, every element of our plan has gone essentially as we expected."

He paused to let his fellow European translate into French. Then he went on, "Of course, the police authorities of every European nation, plus the Americans, are determined to destroy us. What else did we expect? Were they to let us ship thousands of kilos of our particular product into their countries without doing everything they could to stop us? Their politicians thrive on their promises to eliminate our business. We must expect them to put on some show of trying."

"There is talk of an American named Bolan sticking his nose in our business," one Arab said. "My sources say he is a very dangerous man."

"Against crude hill peasants in New York and Los Angeles," Muro replied. "That's all he's ever had to fight—the dimwits of the Cosa Nostra. I don't think Mr. Bolan has ever challenged *our* kind."

"And this woman, Emily Grant...?"

"When we find her, we will send her to you. You may dispose of her in whatever way you wish. She will be yours, I promise you."

The Libyan spoke. "*When* you find her. When you find him. And when will that be, Signor Muro? Last night, this Bolan killed Signor Volte, in the sinking of your ship's launch. Before that, a man, certainly Bolan, sank one of my government's valuable attack boats, with all its crew and a fifty-million-lira shipment of—"

"If," Muro interrupted calmly, "we cannot afford to accept the loss of a gunboat, no matter how modern and sophisticated, plus a single shipment of our merchandise, and perhaps a few men, too, then perhaps we are not men with sufficient courage to engage in the multibillion-lira trade we are establishing. Could that be so, my friends?"

"My president," the Libyan said firmly, angrily, "demands compensation—"

"*Demands!*" Muro shrieked, jumping to his feet. "He *demands*? My friend, you tell your squalid little colonel that Vittorio Muro and his honored associates were doing business all over the world, at immense profit, when he was crawling in the sand, licking the boots of his country's conquerors. He *demands*? With a crook of my little finger, my friend, I can have his security penetrated and his balls cut off and tossed under his nose when next he puts his face to the floor of his mosque for his prayers! He is not dealing now with timid governments afraid he will deny them their oil.

Tell him not to posture with a man like Vittorio Muro, if he values his manhood and his life.''

One of the French-speaking men—no doubt an Iranian, as Emily had guessed—began to protest, but Muro turned and yelled at him in heavily accented French.

"I open your market. I close your market. You make money. You don't make money. *As I decide.* I am not political. My friends and I are wealthy without you. I do not have an atom bomb, you can tell your senile holy man. But I can take off his balls, too. And if he dies I will pack his scrawny corpse in lard and cast it into salt water. He will be unclean, as your superstition has it, and he will never reach paradise. Did I not have one of your most powerful ayatollahs killed, to show you how powerful *I* am? I can have it done again, never fear. And what cowardly bombs will you plant with *me*? Hmm? Do you want to try it?''

"Padrone . . .'' the European said quietly.

"Don't call me that, Jacques. Not now. Not ever.''

"I'm sorry. But these gentlemen are our business associates.''

"So they are.'' Muro resumed his seat, his anger almost spent. "Let them remember that. Let them conduct themselves as businessmen. And let me hear no more of what their unwashed leaders 'demand.'''

The Libyan spoke. "The boat last night was the last one my president has. If they sink another—''

"We will move to other plans,'' Muro replied. "And your colonel will receive what we agreed to pay him for the shipments your boats have carried, which will more than compensate him for his losses. Tell him that. He is being well paid. And tell him to use appropriate respect in future communications with me."

"Last night's shipment went through in spite of all," said the Frenchman, Jacques, apparently trying to calm Muro and put the talk back on a rational note.

"Ah, yes." Muro raised his glass of red wine and sipped. "Yes, it did. A nice profit, for all our pains. And today I sent Giovanna to Saint-Tropez to meet with Thuret and his friends, to receive their report and to advise them fully as to what we know. I sent orders also."

"To find the two Americans at all costs, I hope," the Libyan pressed.

"To kill them, not just find them," said one of the Iranians. "To kill them. To—" He paused, and a crooked smile came to his face. "Of course, Signor Muro did promise the woman alive. I *would* like to have her."

"To hurt us, they must come to us," said Muro, again calm and businesslike. "So far they have made two approaches and have escaped each time, but barely. Another time—"

"How many more times can we afford?" the other Iranian demanded.

"How many can *they*?" Jacques asked. "We took care of their man, Millard."

"*We* took care of him," the Iranian corrected.

"We are partners," Jacques said, "are we not?"

"I have something far more important to discuss," Muro told them. "We have but one factory for refining what you send us into the merchandise that makes our profit. That is a weakness. In the first place, its capacity is limited. But more important, if by some mischance it should be found, we would be without a way to turn your crude, gummy junk into the pure white powder that sells for ten times its weight in gold. What good would opium be if we had no way to refine it into heroin? We are vulnerable in this respect, gentlemen, and we must take steps to eliminate that vulnerability."

"We need another laboratory. My president proposes—"

"I imagine he does," Muro interrupted. "Because he thinks others are fools as big as he is. Tell him no. The new laboratory will not be in Libya. It will be in France. Or perhaps in Italy. What I propose is that all the profit we make from our last shipment be invested in the new laboratory—a fine new facility, well hidden, well fortified, with five times the capacity of the one at Barjols. It must be—"

Emily stiffened. Barjols, he had said. Their laboratory was at Barjols. She wasn't sure where that was; somewhere on the inland side of the Massif, she guessed. But it was vital information. Barjols. Her risk had been justified. If she could somehow get the information back to Bolan. . . .

"But we must have money!" one of the Iranians was crying out in French. "Our cause—"

"Damn your cause!" Muro shouted in French, banging the table with his fist. "For the money to buy a few more rifles and bombs, would you deny our business the investment it needs to increase its profit one

thousand percent? Are all of you as ignorant as you talk?"

The other Iranian spoke to the complaining one. "He is right, Ahmed, he is right. The oil is vulnerable a thousand ways. This, only a hundred ways. Besides, the All Merciful has vouchsafed it into *our* hands, free of the petty pointless squabbling of—"

"Of the honored ones, Mahmet. Let it not be forgotten that—"

"Let them seek their honors in their learning and their wisdom," Mahmet interrupted. "We will seek ours in the way the Prophet showed us. Let us not forget, either, that the Imam has blessed our effort."

"I am silent."

"Then it is agreed to," Muro said. "Another laboratory. Maybe someday a third. Maybe someday, my Libyan friend, even one in Tripoli, when your colonel matures and is a man. If ever that day comes."

Emily crawled backward. There was perhaps more to hear, but the meeting might soon break up, from the sound of this talk, and it was vital that she survive this night to take what she had learned back to Bolan.

She eased open the door between the pantry and the corridor that led out of that wing of the house. She slipped through and eased it shut. There in the corridor she rose to her feet and took a moment to catch a breath.

And she felt a tight grip on her arm.

It was Gaillac. *"Signorina?"*

"Ho fame," she whispered weakly.

He shook his head. He didn't accept the explanation that she was hungry. He reached for the door to the pantry.

With her right hand, which was free, she grabbed the blade from the waistband of the toreador pants and thrust it violently upward, under his ribs and into his lungs. Gaillac grunted and coughed, but even with blood rising in his throat he retained the energy to strike at her. She hit him with an abrupt chop across his throat, then stuck the blade into his throat. Gaillac fell to the floor. And to be certain he was dead, Emily slashed the knife across his throat from ear to ear. She couldn't afford to leave him alive. She watched as the life drained out of him.

Emily hurried cautiously through the halls and up the stairs to her room. She paused outside the door and pulled the length of nylon cord from her bikini bra and looped it around the knob on the bolt. She closed the door with the doubled cord running between the door and the frame, then pulled hard on the two ends of the cord. It didn't work the first time, but she tried it again; and this time the loop pulled the knob toward the door frame and bolted the door. She pulled on one end of the cord, and it slipped through into her hands.

It was an old trick, but it almost always worked. It had in fact worked this afternoon, when she tried it to be sure this door wasn't too tight for it. When Muro arrived, she would be securely locked in her room. And if he guessed she'd dropped from her balcony, he would know she couldn't have climbed back up.

10

"No," Grimmaud said. "Not a word. Nothing un-usual. The *Mistral* left the yacht basin this morning and took up its usual station off Plage de Tahiti, just as it has done every morning this week. Monsieur Thuret is on holiday, I suppose. He spends his days off the beach, his nights in the yacht basin. He brings his daughter ashore for dinner and for dancing each evening. Noth-ing suspicious."

Bolan had told Grimmaud how he went on board the *Mistral*. He had described the conversation he had overheard, particularly the harsh voice of the woman he had been unable to identify.

"The woman's voice," Grimmaud asked, "you are sure it wasn't Mademoiselle Thuret?"

"I'm sure. It was the voice of an older woman."

Grimmaud nodded thoughtfully. "Another wom-an..." he mused.

"Have you ever heard the name Anthony 'Deacon' Dicomano?" Bolan asked.

Grimmaud shook his head.

"Check with RG," Bolan said, referring to Ren-seignements Generaux, the records office of Sûreté.

"And with Interpol. Dicomano was an enforcer. A tough sadistic hit man, with a gruesome record in both Europe and America. RG will have a dossier on him."

" 'Was'? You say 'was' an enforcer?"

Bolan nodded. "Was."

Grimmaud walked to the window of Bolan's hotel room. They had agreed it would be better if he met with Bolan here, not in the dining room, since the question might be raised sooner or later as to the relationship between them. Grimmaud was a plainclothes agent, but someone might recognize him as an agent of Police Judiciare and want to know why he sat and talked with Joseph Robinson, ostensibly a vacant-minded American tourist. He stared down at the swimming pool.

"I assume you had something to do with this past tense," Grimmaud said soberly.

Bolan shrugged. He was eating a breakfast of bacon, eggs, toast and coffee. The French could do an American breakfast if you prodded them.

"If you have any doubt of what I am telling you about Thuret," Bolan said, "consider the fact that he didn't report to the police this morning that he found a corpse with a broken neck on the deck of his yacht sometime after 2:00 a.m. He *didn't* report that, did he?"

"No, he didn't. One could wish to know," he added speculatively, turning away from the window, "what they did with the body. Interesting... No report of the killing. No corpse. They didn't throw it overboard. Interesting that they knew how to dispose of it."

"What's going on aboard the *Mistral* is a lead. What will you do now?"

"I have already placed Monsieur Thuret and his boat under full surveillance. We are conducting a thorough examination of every record we have, to learn everything we can about him—his personal and business history, his employees, his business associates, his tax records—"

"I can't believe Dicomano worked for Thuret," Bolan cut in. "Maybe he worked for Muro and was aboard the *Mistral* to dominate Thuret and keep him in line."

"Tell me something, *monsieur*," Grimmaud said. "When you watched the *Mistral* through your binoculars, was Dicomano on board? Or any female beside Brigitte Thuret?"

Bolan drew a deep breath. "I don't think either of them was on board. I would've noticed. Of course, they could have been below."

"It seems probable," Grimmaud said, "that the woman and Dicomano came aboard together, probably after the boat docked at Saint-Tropez. But the big question, my friend, is who is the woman?"

Bolan shook his head. "That's not the question. The question still is, where's the lab? After that, the question is, how do we get Emily out of the clutches of Muro? I won't sacrifice her."

AT NOON Bolan sat at poolside and had lunch with Yvette. She had changed from her strange purple-and-green one-piece into an equally strange suit of iridescent green ribbons that ran here and there across her body, covering only the minimum that Florida beaches would require be covered, leaving uncovered enough to ensure that every man on every Florida beach would be staring.

Conscious always of the necessity of keeping her slender figure, she nibbled sparingly at a salad.

"Maurice has checked with headquarters again," she told him. "Anthony Dicomano is indeed known well to Renseignements Generaux. They have a heavy dossier on him. He is not, as far as they know, in France. So what should they do with the dossier now? What last entry?"

"They can close the dossier," Bolan said dryly. "Tell them to enter it as an accidental death. Industrial accident, we might say—died of one of the hazards of his employment."

"A small plane from Corsica landed at Nice yesterday afternoon," she went on. "Two passengers were dropped off, and the plane returned to Bastia. The two passengers were a man and a woman. Robert Clary and Carla Plana."

"Whose airplane?"

"It is registered in the name of Calanche & Company, Bastia. Calanche is a firm of import-export brokers, with offices in Bastia and Marseilles."

"A front for Vittorio Muro and Union Corse, do you suppose?" he asked.

"Possibly."

"I want word from Emily," he said. "Losing Millard was bad enough. But to lose Emily Grant, too... It just can't happen."

"Je comprend," she said. She almost never spoke French to him, except when touched with emotion. She lowered her eyes. "Yes, I understand."

At the next table a tall, thin, dark woman talked quietly with a man, and her gaze passed often across Bolan and Yvette, as the warrior had noticed for some time.

"Smile," Bolan whispered to Yvette. "I'm supposed to be a vacationing American businessman who's had the good fortune to get a glamorous French model to sleep with him. We had better work at sustaining the image."

"Which elements of it are difficult to sustain?" Yvette asked coquettishly.

"Not that you're a glamorous Frenchwoman," he replied, saluting her with his glass.

"It is difficult to sustain the image of you as a not-very-bright American businessman. An American, yes. You are an American, and it would be difficult to make anyone suppose otherwise. I'm afraid no one is going to look at you very hard and take you for a manufacturer of... What is the American term? Of 'widgets.' A manufacturer of widgets."

"Thank you," Bolan said. "But seriously, I think someone is watching us."

"Someone in particular?"

"Yes. The woman in black over there."

Yvette glanced at the tall, dark woman. "Staring at the swimming suit, I suspect."

Bolan sipped wine and at last began to eat the meal he'd been toying with.

The tall woman summoned the waiter. *"Apportez le café maintenant, s'il vous plaît. Et...qu'est-ce que vous avez comme fruit?"*

Bolan stiffened. "Listen to her!"

"Qu'est-ce vous avez comme fromage?" the woman asked.

"The accent!" Bolan whispered to Yvette. "Odd French, isn't it?"

She shrugged. "Italian," she said. "She speaks French with an Italian accent."

The woman's voice was harsh, too. Could it be the voice he had heard from the cabin of the *Mistral* last night? He strained to listen to her, but the woman leaned across her table and returned to her quiet conversation with her companion. Bolan could hear nothing more.

"Let's find out who she is. And the man. How fast can you get word to Grimmaud?"

"Is it important?"

"It could be."

"Very well. Police Judiciare will check the hotel register cards."

WHEN THE MAN AND WOMAN finished their coffee and fruit, Yvette left the table, circled the pool and entered the hotel. The man left the table, heading in the other direction, toward the lobby. Bolan followed him.

The short, heavyset man proceeded through the hotel and out into the parking lot, where he got into a maroon Renault. Bolan hurried to the BMW and prepared to follow.

The man drove the Renault down from the hill and onto the highway out of Saint-Tropez. Bolan kept a distance behind and hoped the man wouldn't notice the tail. The warrior was adept at pursuit, but if this man knew the area well, then Bolan would easily be shaken off.

The single highway out of Saint-Tropez shortly meets an intersection with highways to the west, toward Le Lavandou and Toulon, and to the east, toward Saint-Raphaël and Cannes. But the maroon Renault took neither of these; it entered the winding country road that climbs into the forests of the Maures Massif. The man drove purposefully, never slowing to look at the breathtaking scenery. He crossed the ridge of the Massif and turned onto the Autoroute at Le Luc. On the Autoroute he picked up speed until he was doing seventy-five mph. Bolan remained close behind. If the man was trying to outrun him, he didn't have the car for it.

The Renault left the Autoroute at the Brignoles exit. Bolan nearly missed that turn, since he was keeping almost half a mile between his vehicle and the Renault. But he saw it in time and followed.

Once more the Renault sped purposefully along a winding country road. They were now in the rural, hilly part of southern France that lay behind the Massif: a countryside of farms, vineyards and woods. The man driving the Renault passed rapidly through the picturesque little market town of Barjols. Just north of Barjols, he turned into a narrow country lane that wound into a forest and rose along a hillside.

Bolan dropped back farther. Unless the man in the Renault was completely oblivious, he'd fix his attention now on any car following him. And he'd surely recognize the BMW that had pulled away from the Byblos Hotel shortly after he did. Bolan lost sight of the Renault. There were private lanes, blocked by gates on both sides of the road. It would be easy for the Renault to disappear down one of those before Bolan caught up and saw the driver close the gate behind him—which was just what happened.

BOLAN WAS BACK at the Byblos by four-thirty. Yvette was still working, but when she saw him she broke off the photo session and hurried over. For appearances she kissed him, then grabbed a black beach coat that went with the sarong outfit she wore, covered herself and beckoned him to follow her inside.

"We have a little information about a lady with the Italian accent," she announced. "It's important."

"I thought it might be," he said as he followed her along the tiled hallway toward the door of his room.

When they were inside, she went to the window, looked down at the pool then turned to him. "She is very likely—it's not sure by any means—but it seems likely she is Giovanna Sestri, a sister-in-law of Vittorio Muro."

"Nice coincidence."

"We're not sure," Yvette warned. "She is registered at the hotel under another name. She flew into Nice from Corsica yesterday afternoon on a private plane belonging to Calanche & Company. She was accompanied by a man that fits your description of Anthony Dicomano. He is registered here, too, under another name. He did not sleep in his room last night."

"Who was the man who had lunch with her?"

Yvette shrugged.

"I followed him. How quickly can we get a helicopter?"

IT WOULD HAVE BEEN UNWISE for them to be seen boarding a Police Judiciare helicopter at the Saint-Tropez heliport, so Bolan and Yvette drove a few miles to Cavalière, where the helicopter waited for them in a field. It was before six, and when the helicopter lifted off they still had plenty of time before sunset. Bolan had a Michelin highway map on his lap. While Yvette drove the BMW to Cavalière, he had marked the highways over which he had driven that afternoon.

Urgent though their mission was, it was impossible to overlook the spectacular beauty of the Riviera coast, then of the Maures Massif, as they banged along in the chopper, never rising more than a thousand meters above the variegated landscape.

The helicopter required only twenty-five minutes to reach the mountain village of Barjols. There the police pilot flew a series of lazy circles, to let Bolan peer intently at the roads and try to identify the ones he'd traveled while following the Renault. The highway intersection to the north of the town was easy enough to recognize. North of that there were only two lanes he might have taken. His attention had been on the Renault a few hours earlier, not on landmarks; but he managed after a few minutes' circling to identify the lane he felt certain the Renault had taken. The pilot dipped lower and followed the lane north.

To the north was the valley of the Verdon River, a few kilometers to the east of what was called the Grand Canyon of the Verdon, which offered some of the most beautiful scenery in France. Directly under the helicopter lay a range of wooded hills, some of them the sites for luxurious villas. Bolan had brought the binoculars and began to scan the courtyards of villas, looking for the Renault.

It wasn't difficult to find. The maroon vehicle was drawn up before a low, modern house with windows that overlooked a gorgeous view of woods and hills. The house was big, and behind it stood several outbuildings, ostensibly a barn, what looked to be a guest house and a garage. Half a dozen cars and two vans were parked close together, all but the Renault and a Mercedes being pulled into two groves, to conceal them from any but close observation from the air.

The helicopter drew attention. Looking through the binoculars, Bolan found himself face-to-face with other binoculars: men staring up at the helicopter and at him.

"Enough," he said to the pilot. "Let's get out of here before they're thoroughly alerted. Make a point of flying low over two or three other villas. Maybe we can make them think we weren't interested in them."

"You think it's the laboratory?" Yvette asked.

"Who knows?" said Bolan. "It could be. That's our next job—to find out."

11

"I have interesting news for you," Inspector Grimmaud announced when Bolan and Yvette returned from their helicopter flight. They met in the garage of a car rental agency in Saint-Tropez. "The *Mistral* did not return to the yacht basin this evening. It's gone. We don't know where. Missing, you might say."

"Can't you track it down?" Bolan asked. "After all, a yacht isn't that small. Where could you hide one?"

Grimmaud shook his head. "Not so easy. Once darkness falls, there are a thousand small yachts at sea along the Riviera coast—as you learned when you and Yvette went to sea—and who knows which one...?" He favored Bolan with a Gallic shrug. "On the other hand, we have an idea. The navy reports that the *Santa Margherita* left Bastia late this afternoon. These two facts may be unrelated, but..." He shrugged again. "It is possible they may be meeting at sea."

"No word of Dicomano?" Bolan asked. "Nobody's asked about him?"

Grimmaud shook his head. "No. On the other hand, we have interesting news about the woman who was registered at the Byblos Hotel as Carla Plana. We photographed her surreptitiously and wired the photographs to Paris. No problem. No question. She is Giovanna Sestri, as we suspected—Vittorio Muro's sister-in-law. What is more, she is gone. She paid her account in cash and checked out of the hotel this afternoon. A suggestive fact, no?''

"Didn't you tail her?" Bolan asked. "Should have been a simple job."

"Yes, but with one agent only. The lady is clever. She seemed to find little difficulty in discovering she was being followed, then in evading her follower."

"The private plane that brought her in from Corsica...?" Bolan suggested.

"We're watching for that."

"Any idea where the *Santa Margherita* is going?"

"Not yet. The navy is watching. It is on a northwest course, perhaps returning to Saint-Tropez. It is under intense surveillance. *It* will not escape us."

"Who's on board? Is there any way to tell?"

"A navy helicopter flew over the yacht just before sunset. The pilot reports that a young woman, naked, was playing a guitar on the rear deck."

"Emily Grant?" Yvette asked.

Another Gallic shrug. "There is no way to know. How many yachts in this area have naked girls on deck? Half of them?"

"If that's Emily, just where is he taking her?" Bolan wondered.

THE YACHT WAS TAKING Vittorio Muro and a dozen dangerous-looking men to Saint-Tropez. Emily had been confined to her cabin while some mysterious cargo was loaded aboard. It wasn't morphine base, nothing so light and so compact as that. Artillery was what she suspected—a load of heavy arms. And the dozen men were soldiers. She was surprised that something secret and mysterious was being loaded on the vessel. The padrone wasn't known for taking risks. Obviously something important was happening.

Vittorio Muro was angry, so angry that he hadn't gone to her room the previous night. The sour-faced woman had come to check, to make certain that the Texas whore—as she called her—was indeed locked in her room. It was only in the morning, when Muro himself came to let her out, that she was told that a trusted, valued servant had been murdered in the villa during the night.

"Pierre Gaillac, a very trusted business associate," Muro had complained. "An experienced man quite capable of defending himself. I must believe he was murdered by a trained assassin. You did not, I suppose, have any occasion to be outside on your balcony last night?"

Emily's breath caught. "Why...why, no. I waited for you, *signor*, then fell asleep. When morning came, I woke and was surprised to find myself alone, and locked in."

"So you could not have seen anyone suspicious on the grounds below your window? You did not look out? You saw no one out there?"

"*Signor*, I looked out my window. Of course I did. The night was beautiful. I stood on the balcony for a time. I saw men about in the courtyard, but I saw no one who looked suspicious to me, no one but your men, who I expected to see. And all of them looked calm. None seemed excited about anything.''

He smiled a wry, lopsided smile. "But who would you identify as suspicious?" he asked rhetorically. "No, I am afraid the killer could have walked up and kissed you on the cheek and you would not have suspected him." Muro sighed. "I seem to be under siege, my dear. When we return to Saint-Tropez, I will have to surrender the pleasure of your company. In the meanwhile, let's share a bit of breakfast on the terrace. Even in such times, a man must take food and drink."

Breakfast took a long time. Even though the padrone seemed anxious to give some of his attention to her and to his meal, he was constantly interrupted by grim men who hurried up to speak a quiet word in his ear and receive a quiet word in return. He was, over that breakfast, the image of a powerful man in a testing time.

In her experience Emily had seen powerful men tested—in government and business—and she knew the symptoms. Something was wrong for Vittorio Muro. Dared she hope it was something being done by Mack Bolan? Dared she hope his concern was for something more than what *she* had done?

It was during that extended breakfast that she overheard talk from which she understood that Pierre Gaillac wasn't the only trusted associate of Muro's who had died overnight. As near as she could tell, someone had been killed back in mainland France. She overheard the name Bolan. If they didn't know he was at work, they at least suspected it.

"Have you ever heard the name Mack Bolan?"

"The name seems familiar, *signor*. But I cannot..."

"It is the name of a notorious American killer," Muro told her. "I have reason to believe he has been hired to kill me."

"Signor!"

Muro made a calming gesture, a flutter of his hand. "No matter. He was not here last night. My friend Gaillac was killed by someone else, probably by someone I trust, perhaps over some question of honor or rivalry. I have one further question, Linda. Did Gaillac approach you? I mean, did he suggest he would like to spend the evening in your room with you, while I was finishing my business conference?"

"No, *signor*," she replied. "When he was with me, he was very respectful."

Muro nodded. "Yes, I would not have thought it of Gaillac."

"I wish I could help, *signor*. I wish I had seen something that would be helpful."

Muro turned down the corners of his mouth and again nodded, this time more emphatically. "Do not worry, Linda. I am more than capable of handling this Mack Bolan."

So he said. But Muro was angry and concerned. And he was marshaling his forces.

EMILY AND MURO had returned to the *Santa Margherita* in the afternoon, and once again Emily was locked in her cabin with shackles on her ankles—put on her this time by an embarrassed member of the crew.

When the mysterious cargo was loaded, the same man returned, unlocked the leg irons and told her the padrone wished her to remain in her cabin until seven o'clock, at which time she was to join him for cocktails on the rear deck. She was to bring her guitar, he told her, and to dress in the way she knew the padrone liked. He winked, meaning, of course, that they both understood she was to appear in just half a bikini, with perhaps a jacket over her shoulders.

So dressed, she strummed the guitar and sipped the wine Muro offered her as he made a conspicuous but inadequate effort to relax. The threat of Bolan troubled him more than he was ready to acknowledge. He was distant, preoccupied, but he bade her sing and play for him; and from time to time he glanced up and smiled at her.

"You drink little, Linda," he said. "I had supposed Texans drank heavily. Is it not the sweetish American whiskey, bourbon, that is favored in Texas?"

"Would you be pleased with me, *signor*, if I got drunk and could neither play nor entertain you otherwise?" she asked with mock innocence. "Anyway, I would wager you have no bourbon aboard *Santa Margherita*."

Vittorio Muro regarded her for a moment with shrewd, appraising eyes. Then he smiled. "You are different, Linda," he said. "Not like the others. I have two options with you. One, to put you off my yacht and out of my life as soon as possible, the other, to keep you with me and develop a more complete appreciation of you. You would not like to commit yourself to me, would you? I mean to say, you do have your future planned, don't you?"

She responded cautiously. "I do, *signor*. But not so firmly that I could not change my mind."

"Ah, Linda…" he sighed. "Take off the rest of your clothes while you make music for me. I want to see all of you. Let my imagination play."

GUESSING that a confrontation might develop within the next twenty-four hours, Mack Bolan took the time to check his weapons. They weren't what he might have wished for. This operation would depend on *him*, on his skills, experience and instincts, not on the weapons.

He couldn't depend on the assistance of the French police and military, either. They were too anxious to move. From the looks of the situation, he was going to have to rescue Emily, either from the yacht or maybe even from the lab itself, if that was where they were taking her, before he set to work to blast a fatal hole in the new heroin alliance. And that kind of operation called for one man. If he couldn't secure the cooperation of the French in standing aside until Emily was safe, then maybe he would have to get the jump on them.

He sat in the BMW after Grimmaud had left, and he and Yvette examined his arsenal.

The Beretta Model 12 was an ugly submachine gun, a little awkward in the hands. There was nothing sophisticated about it; all it could do was bark out short bursts of 9 mm bullets, at a rate of about nine per second. The long magazines held forty rounds, meaning that a magazine held maybe eight half-second bursts. If you wanted to spray a lot of fire, you would go through a magazine in two or three bursts. All he had was five magazines. He would have to be damned selective about his shooting.

He had five clips for the Lahti, the handsome Finnish pistol the French had also supplied. That meant he had forty rounds. Also, he had the Luger with one extra clip. The Lahti was sound-suppressed; the Luger wasn't.

Finally, he had two grenades, British-manufactured hand bombs.

"Do I dare venture a suggestion?" Yvette asked.

Bolan nodded, still checking the action of the Lahti. It was smooth.

"Emotion is getting in the way, Mack," she said.

"Meaning...?"

"Meaning that you've struck heavy blows against the Shiite-Corsican alliance—with our help—but that now you're thinking of doing something utterly foolish because Emily Grant is their prisoner. We—"

"I don't let good people get killed if I can prevent it," Bolan snapped. "Do you?"

"Mack... How can I help?"

"By keeping out of my way, Yvette. More than that, by keeping all your friends out of my way until Emily is safe. That element of what we have to do is my problem. After I solve that, we can work together."

"You ask much of your friends."

A SUMMER STORM crossed the Mediterranean not long after sunset, and by ten o'clock the *Santa Margherita* was rolling in six-foot seas, its white rigging gleaming from time to time in the eerie blue light of long lightning flashes. Great bolts flew across the sky from cloud to cloud. The wind was fresh and cool and smelled of distant rain.

The padrone hadn't yet elected to go below out of the storm. He sat still at his table, calmly sipping wine, more content it seemed with the stormy night than he'd been with the placid evening that had gone before. Emily sat with him, huddled now against the wind, her beach coat closed around her, but like him fascinated with the display of lightning. They were alike in that respect, at least.

ON THE *MISTRAL* the storm wasn't taken so calmly. The little yacht was lifted high on the six-foot seas, then plunged sickeningly into the troughs, its decks awash as the bow split an onrushing wave and plunged through it. All hatches were tightly secured. A pump spewed water from the bilge. Everyone huddled in the main cabin, listening to the storm, feeling the vessel list, wondering if it could ride out the storm or if it would be caught sideways and turned over.

A crewman was at the inside bridge, laboriously working the wheel and throttles, keeping the bow against the oncoming seas. Grimly weaving on their chairs in the lounge behind, everyone else was nauseous and apprehensive.

Robert Thuret chewed and smoked a rapidly diminishing Havana cigar. He was an emaciated, pallid man, his long face deeply lined with vertical wrinkles, his lips thin and blue. His daughter, Brigitte, sat stiffly, glancing around, seeming to hear every gurgle of water that broke through the closed hatches and doors, frightened by every sound.

Two men sat at the table in the center of the lounge—one French by the look of him, one clearly Middle Eastern, and in fact an Iranian. A woman sat in a deep chair toward the rear of the lounge. She was Giovanna Sestri, the sister-in-law of Vittorio Muro, an angry-looking woman with gray-streaked black hair, a leathery mannish face, a hard mannish body. She glanced at the others in turn. She was terrified, but she hated the fear on the faces of her companions, and she tried to show them scorn. She sipped wine and pretended she felt nothing. Let them think so. It was part of her long-practiced persona to show no fear in any situation.

"We can never make the transfer," Thuret said. "Even if we don't sink before we find the *Santa Margherita*..."

"Shut up," Giovanna Sestri gritted through clenched teeth.

IN THE THIN END of Emily's guitar case was a small compartment intended to hold picks, extra strings and whatever other small supplies the player might want to carry. It was only four inches square, but it had a false bottom. Beneath the false bottom was a hidden compartment, just big enough to contain a tiny loaf of C-4 plastique, less than half a kilo. It was enough to create a loud diversionary explosion, or to blow a hole in the hull of a yacht.

A tiny radio receiver was taped to the package of plastique, powered by the same kind of paper-thin battery that is contained in every package of Polaroid SX-70 film to power the camera. The receiver was tuned to the frequency of a tiny transmitter hidden inside the guitar itself.

Emily had inserted three thin flexible steel blades in the purple lining. Each was about ten inches long. The end that was flat and dull served as the handle. These blades were meant to be carried inside a person's clothes, just as the one last night had fitted nicely and invisibly into the waistband of the toreador pants Muro had required her to wear. Her problem tonight was that the only clothes she had aboard the *Santa Margherita* were two tiny, tight bikinis and two beach coats. The clothing barely concealed her, let alone a blade or anything else. She had nowhere to carry her blades, except in the guitar case, and it would be awkward to extract them.

About midnight she became aware that the yacht had slowed and was changing course. She switched off the light in her cabin and peered out into the darkness on the sea. The storm had subsided. There was no lightning now to identify the horizon, and the yacht no longer listed as it had before. But the *Santa Margherita* was turning, moving ever slower. She could feel the diminished rotations of the propeller shafts.

Knuckles rapped on the door. The crewman who had shackled her in the afternoon entered her cabin. "I regret it, *mademoiselle*," he said softly, "but I have orders to restrain you once again. It is only for a short time. I know you do understand."

He knelt before her, and once again she submitted to having the oversize handcuffs locked on her ankles.

It had become worse than boring. The chain between the big cuffs was about ten inches long—eight links, she had counted. The steel circles around her ankles were cold at first, then gradually warmed from the heat of her body. She could hobble to her bathroom and back, could, in fact, have hobbled to the upper decks, tortuously. She wondered how many young women had submitted to this over the years and had then taken their generous allotment of money and left the yacht and never told what they had endured there.

Emily sat on her bunk, dressed in a tight, shiny bikini, staring thoughtfully at her chains. She'd had enough! This time she would know why she was chained.

She knew how to get the irons off. She'd slipped out of handcuffs before. These weren't the complex ones she'd worn one night. These were police shackles, meant to be worn by prisoners who were generally observed in custody, not prisoners who were left alone. She used nothing more complex than a hairpin, thoughtfully provided in her bathroom, probably left by one of her many predecessors as the padrone's plaything. It took her no more than two minutes to be free of the shackles. But that was only the beginning.

Opening the door of the cabin was something else. That lock took almost ten minutes, working patiently with the same hairpin, with a guitar pick and with the tip of one of the blades from her guitar case. In time, though, she swung the door open and looked up and down the corridor.

In her hand was the little bomb of C-4 plastique. It was small, but it would serve her purpose.

Emily knew where the engine room was—along the corridor toward the stern, then through a door and down a half flight of steel stairs into the hot, oily, gray-painted, rumbling chamber that contained the big diesels that powered the vessel. The engine room was deserted. No one went there other than to service the engines or to check them. She was able to descend and walk between the two enormous throbbing engines without being seen, her bare feet finding purchase difficult on the steel floor.

Blowing a little hole in the steel hull of the *Santa Margherita* hadn't impressed her as a way to destroy the padrone. The plastique she carried wasn't enough to sink the yacht, except maybe with exceptional luck. What she was looking for in the engine room was a way to cripple the power system, to make the vessel helpless in the water. She didn't know what she would achieve by doing that, but it was all she could do, and she would take her chances with it.

She studied the layout of the engine room. The two big diesels were surely impervious to major damage from her little package of explosives. The fuel supply... That was it! The tanks of diesel fuel were under the steel plates of the engine-room deck. She identified the fuel lines coming up from under those plates—the *Santa Margherita*'s points of vulnerability.

Emily lifted one of the plates and uncovered the tanks, knowing she didn't have much time. She tapped the tanks to see if she could hear which one was full, then taped the plastique to the one that rang more solid than the other.

When the crewman returned to unlock her leg irons, she lay on her bunk reading, her ankles securely chained. The padrone, he told her, would see her again in his cabin. Emily took her guitar with her and made her way to Vittorio Muro's luxurious suite.

WHILE EMILY WAS supposedly shackled in her cabin the yacht had effected a successful rendezvous with the *Mistral*, and Giovanna Sestri was now on board. She had conferred with Muro for thirty minutes and had retired to her cabin. She'd told him that Tony Dicomano had been murdered on the yacht in the basin at Saint-Tropez, and he'd related to her how Pierre Gaillac had been found dead in one of the hallways of the villa.

"I would have suspected the girl from Texas," he'd said to his sister-in-law, "except *she* couldn't be Bolan. And—"

"Bolan is said to be accompanied by a woman operative," Giovanna replied. "This girl—"

"She's a toy," Muro said dismissively. "Fluff, with a lovely body. Last night, when Gaillac was killed, she was locked in her room. She could've climbed down from her balcony, I suppose, but she could never have climbed back up. Anyway, Gaillac was killed by a strong man, who stabbed him to death. She couldn't have done it."

"You invariably underestimate women, brother," Giovanna Sestri said dryly.

12

Bolan drove up through the Massif once more, this time well after midnight. It would be the third time in twelve hours that he'd visited the country road north of Barjols. He wanted to scout the villa in the wooded hills, this time in the early-morning darkness.

He followed the roads he'd driven during the afternoon, the same ones he'd flown over a few hours later in the police helicopter. In the deep darkness of the night they were difficult to find. He made two or three wrong turns, but by 3:00 a.m. he was on the road that led to the villa and was able to identify the inconspicuous lane the maroon Renault had turned onto. Bolan parked the BMW to the side of the road, as much out of sight as possible. He hunkered down beside the car and changed into his camouflage fatigues and covered his face with combat cosmetics.

The warrior got out of the car, jumped the drainage ditch and began to make his way through the woods, paralleling the lane, toward the cluster of house and outbuildings.

A storm had broken over the Massif, stabbing the night with intermittent blue-and-orange flashes. Rain pelted the ground. As far as Bolan was concerned, the storm was good fortune. It would drive the guards to cover and provide the warrior with some light that might permit him to see the defenses.

Bolan was on his own ground now. This was what he knew how to do as well as any man alive. He hurried forward over soggy ground, wondering if he were breaking any beam, tripping any wire that was invisible in the gloom. He was packing his two pistols—the Lahti in sideleather, the Luger in a pocket. The Beretta submachine gun remained in the trunk of the car. It would be an error to kill anyone tonight. A dead body would put everyone in the house on alert—not just tonight, but for days, even weeks.

He worked his way forward through the dripping woods. The land sloped upward, not steeply but with hard rock outcroppings here and there. The ground between the rocks was slippery, and the mud was thin and slick. From time to time he stopped and waited for a flash of lightning to illuminate the way ahead.

The trees and brush were in leaf at this time of year, and he'd moved a considerable distance before he spotted artificial light—an electric light gleaming from the window of a building. He guessed the road and the car were a hundred yards or so behind him, the light about the same distance ahead. The light disappeared behind foliage as he continued moving forward, and once again he was in the dark.

A long, pulsing flash of lightning glared blue-white on the woods for a full two seconds, and he saw the lay of the land ahead in the pelting rain. Brush had been cut from the woods; the land under the trees lay open to anyone watching. Ahead, maybe another fifty yards, a low fence stretched along the border between the woods and a trimmed lawn. Beyond twenty or thirty yards of grass lay a low house and several outbuildings. Thunder rumbled over the hillside, and the sky was again dark.

Bolan crept toward the fence. When the next bolt of lightning lit up the sky, he was within fifteen or twenty feet of the fence and had an unobstructed view of it. The fence was only five feet high, but the insulators on the posts told him it was electrified and not just with the few volts needed to turn cattle. It was high voltage, far more than was needed to protect the innocent.

The lane from the road was to his left. It passed through the electric fence at a gate guarded by at least one man in a dimly lighted guardhouse almost hidden by two big oaks. The main house was directly ahead, the center of the cluster. The maroon Renault stood in front of the house. To the left was a garage. Bolan could see a small gray van parked inside the open doors. To the right was a long low building, the one Bolan guessed was the lab. It was lighted, as was the house. Someone was working.

Through the windows of the house he could see people moving, but they were too distant to be identified without the binoculars, and he hadn't brought those with him. The windows of the lab were covered, though the light shone through. The storm had no doubt driven the sentries inside; he guessed there were hardmen who usually patrolled the fence. He was surprised there were no sensors in the woods—or maybe he'd just been lucky enough to miss them.

He crawled on his belly, examining the ground beneath him as he moved forward, looking for wires. They could be buried shallow, under nothing more than an inch of rotting leaves. He found nothing, and he approached the fence.

Abruptly, as he snaked forward, the grounds around the house, as well as the whole fence line and the first twenty yards outside the fence, came alive with bright white light. He had, beyond any question, crawled onto a sensor. Men burst from the front door of the house and from a door of the building he'd taken for a lab, carrying submachine guns. The gunners formed a sort of skirmish line and advanced toward the fence, weapons held up and ready.

Bolan lay quietly, confident that his camouflage would hide him. He was within the perimeter of the bright light, but he wasn't spotted immediately. He remained pressed to the ground. It was possible that they might decide a dog had tripped the sensor, or some other animal—or anything else they could think of that would relieve them of having to search the whole perimeter in this storm.

Lightning played across the sky, outlining the tall thunderhead that generated it. The thunder cracked like an immense pistol shot, then roared. The air was alive with the distinctive sharp odor of electricity.

Surging wind drove rain across the lights. A gust blew cold water on a hot light, and the bulb blew. Glass showered to the ground, and smoke drifted away on the wind. The hardmen stiffened, then saw something and relaxed.

"Une grosse branche!" someone yelled. Fortunately, the man was assuming that a branch, blown down by the wind, had fallen on the sensor.

None of them were anxious to stay out in the rain and wind, not to mention the threatening lightning. The explanation was accepted, and one by one, glancing back, they filed back into the house and the lab.

Bolan remained flat against the ground, unseen. This time he'd been lucky.

All right. The sensors—this one at least—detected pressure. They were buried in the ground, then, like land mines. A falling limb wouldn't have triggered anything more sophisticated, like one of the new beams that were sensitive only to movement by a warm body.

The hardmen weren't as formidable as they thought, and obviously had no idea what technology could do, had no idea that instruments could detect the unique magnetic signal that emanated from a human body and not confuse it with the signal from a skunk.

Bolan backed off, carefully crawling back over the ground he'd previously covered. He had tripped one alarm without being caught, but he couldn't do it again. The next time the hardmen ventured into the rain they'd stay out, storm or no storm. He decided to try the lane. If approaching cars didn't set off sensors, then it was likely the alliance depended on human vigilance—human vigilance and the fence.

Anyway, he still wanted to know as much as he could about this place. Was this indeed the heroin lab he was looking for? Or just the headquarters of some French conspiracy? Knowing what he did of French politics, he could have stumbled on the Riviera station of the GIGN—Groupe d'Intervention de la Gendarmerie Nationale. If so, it was entirely possible that Grimmaud and Yvette—or indeed the entire apparatus of Police Judiciare—wouldn't know about it. That was how the French operated. Even Monsieur le Président de la République didn't know much about GIGN. If, in fact, he knew anything.

All the sensors were near the fence, apparently, so Bolan backed away with no trouble, then slipped to his left to the border of the lane between the road and the gate.

It was an unpaved estate lawn, curving up and around the hill toward the house. The middle of the lane, he guessed, would be free of sensors. He walked cautiously up the center.

Presently the house was in view again. The floodlights had been left blazing. Good enough. Bolan edged into the drainage ditch at the right side of the road. Crouching, he worked his way forward toward the gate.

The guardhouse had been constructed under two large trees, so it wouldn't be visible from the air, just as the fence didn't run openly across the land but was concealed from the air by running along the line of brush that marked the treeline.

As the warrior crept nearer he recognized the incessant rhythms and nasal tones of Middle-Eastern music flowing from the guardhouse. Someone was listening to Radio Cairo or Radio Damascus. No matter what they were paid or how they were punished or how well they understood what they were guarding, it was difficult for sentries to stand or sit hour after hour on alert. They smoked, listened to radios, read magazines, did anything they could to relieve their boredom. The man who was listening to the music wouldn't be able to hear a soldier slipping through the woods toward his post.

Bolan approached the gate and the guard shack just as a spectacular burst of lightning erupted overhead and the night shook with thunder. Under the cover of that boom, he rushed the gate and the guardhouse and ran through.

Rain penetrated his clothes. Bolan wasn't insensitive to rain and cold, and as he crawled along the fence line, this time inside, he shivered from the chilling water that had seeped through to his skin. Now, the question was, were there sensors in the smooth lawn, inside the fence that was supposed to protect the house and outbuildings from any intrusion? If there were, he'd have to shoot his way out—two pistols against a score of burp guns in the hands, very likely, of unthinking fanatics.

He crawled toward the building he took for the laboratory, which was his primary target.

The lawn was less than fifty yards across, and he covered it quickly, once he'd decided that crawling along and feeling the turf for sensors wasn't productive. If there were sensors here, they would be beam type, and would sense warmth and movement or maybe his magnetic field. In a crouch, he trotted over the last few yards to the wall of the building.

The windows were covered by drapes, but he could tell which rooms were lighted and which weren't. He would break into one of the dark rooms.

Bolan rounded the building to the right and reached a window on the far end. The room beyond was dark, so he put his ear to the glass and listened. Nothing. Then he applied pressure to the glass, at first gently, then with more force. The glass yielded reluctantly—it bent, then cracked. Large shards dropped to the floor inside with only a minor clatter. If there had been someone in the room immediately behind that window, an alarm would have been raised. But no one was there, and the glass fell unheard. The occupants were confident of the building's security. Nothing prevented Bolan from climbing in.

The room he entered was a storeroom, stacked with bundles and barrels. The smell was unmistakable—the biting stench of acetic acid. Acetic anhydride was one of the chemicals that converted morphine base into high-grade, undiluted heroin.

Bolan made himself a hidey-hole by moving three of the barrels. He pressed himself to a door, ready to spring behind the barrels if need be. He listened. No sound. Cautiously he opened the door and looked into the next room.

And saw the laboratory-factory, the biggest heroin-manufacturing lab Bolan had ever encountered. Other labs he'd destroyed usually amounted to a table or two, with burners, cans and vats, often crude and dirty. This one had been put together from the beginning as an industrial laboratory for a single purpose: conversion of a raw product into a refined poison. Instead of a bathtub filled with chemicals, this lab had glistening glassware, connected by tubes and hoses. There was no crude charcoal heater; this lab featured clean Bunsen burners, fueled from cylinders of propane. The big room was tidy and clean.

It was relatively easy to refine the raw opium—the gummy secretion from the poppy pods—into morphine base. Refining the base into heroin was a far more complex task, requiring skilled chemists. That was why the final step was done in Europe and not in the rude countries where the poppies grew. Each poppy produced only a minute amount of the gum, and it took twelve kilos of that substance to make a kilo of morphine base. The morphine base, however, would convert into heroin at a ratio of one to one. A laboratory factory this big could refine enough heroin to feed an epidemic of addiction.

Alchemists had spent centuries searching for the "philosopher's stone," the reagent that would turn lead to gold. The profit to be expected from turning lead to gold was nothing compared to what was realistically to be expected from turning opium to heroin. The trade here depended on two things: a constant supply of morphine base already refined out of raw opium, plus an equivalent supply of the needed chemicals. The only other ingredient was technicians with a total lack of human decency. No one in the trade cared that the substance they created destroyed human lives.

If the bubonic plague was called "the black death," this was surely "the white death"—with the difference being that the real rats carried one while human rats carried the other.

Bolan was tempted to destroy what he saw, perhaps by starting a fire that would eliminate as much as a million dollars' worth of narcotics. But that would only serve to alert Muro's alliance that Mack Bolan or someone else had broken the security of his French laboratory. What was more, loss of the lab wouldn't stop them. He had to do more than burn down their factory.

Thunder rattled the windows of the laboratory. A door opened, and two men in white lab coats ran in out of the pelting rain, laughing and wiping water off their faces. They were so distracted that they didn't notice the man standing in the shadows, and Bolan was able to back out of their lab and close the door, unseen. It had been close, though, and in the storeroom, crouching behind the barrels, he shivered and was again conscious that he was soaked with cold rainwater.

No matter. The warrior had work to do. He emerged from behind the barrels, returned to the window he'd broken and peered out. No one was outside. He climbed out into the driving rain, conscious of the falling numbers. The stormy sky was beginning to change from black to gray. After lightning silhouetted the hills surrounding the estate, they didn't disappear into darkness but remained faintly visible. Dawn was imminent. He sprinted across the lawn to the house. Pressing against the wall, thankful for the shelter of the eaves above him, Bolan moved from one window to another, trying to gather whatever intel he could.

He decided he wouldn't risk entering the house. Even so, he gained an impression of how it was laid out. A wing at the back contained the kitchen. A paved walkway connected the kitchen and the lab. The number of garbage cans behind the kitchen suggested that twenty or more people were living in the house. Chemists. Hardmen. Probably drivers. The house was lighted. He couldn't see through the crack between the curtained windows, but he could see moving shadows as figures passed between windows and lamps.

The kitchen door, ten feet behind him, opened. Bolan froze, pressed flat against the wall. A man stepped outside, carrying a paper bag. He jerked the lid off one of the cans and dropped the garbage inside. After jamming the lid back on, he stood on the porch and drew deep breaths, looking at the storm. The man wore a black burnoose, a beige double-breasted suit with white shirt buttoned tight under his chin but no necktie. His gun belt pinched in the suit jacket at his waist. A heavy automatic hung on his hip. His glance passed over Bolan, but he didn't see him. The Arab yawned, turned and went back inside.

For Bolan it was time to go. The light of dawn was coming on too fast. Soon the shadows would no longer provide cover. He slipped around the corner of the building and walked along the edge of the driveway toward the gate.

He had slipped past the guardhouse once. He'd have to do it again. He approached the little shack under the big trees. It was lighted. The warrior crept forward and risked a look inside. Another black burnoose. The compound was guarded by Shiites. The radio still blared Arabic music, and Burnoose sat awake, smoking, no more alert than he had been earlier. Bolan crawled around the guardhouse, keeping close to the ground. He backed away and watched Burnoose for a moment. The man yawned and squinted toward the house. Bolan slipped through the gate and sprinted down the lane.

Running through the rain with the thunder rumbling overhead, Bolan almost failed to hear the maroon Renault behind him. He was alerted by the yellow glare of headlights reflected from the wet leaves ahead, and just in time he threw himself into the ditch by the side of the road. He drew the Lahti from its holster, expecting the car to stop, and was surprised when it didn't. Whoever was driving was in a hurry, driving fast, unskillfully fighting the unpaved lane, letting the car skid and lurch while struggling to hold it.

Bolan trotted to the end of the lane and turned to the left onto the country road where he'd left his vehicle. The sky had turned light gray. The rain was slackening, and the lightning was more distant and less spectacular, the thunder a growling roll. He walked south on the road, around a gentle curve and caught sight of his car. . . .

Which was flanked by two men in burnooses, each with a burp gun cradled under his arm. Bolan launched himself toward the ditch, then slithered up to the edge of the woods.

Okay. This was his game, his kind of warfare. He circled the woods, silent, deadly, checking to the rear to be sure no more Iranians lay in ambush. There were none. These hardmen were fanatic believers, confident of themselves and of the benevolent providence that would give them victory, simply as a gift. Elementary infantry tactics weren't necessary for men whose triumph was preordained. They would kill. That was all. They would kill, as they always had. And if they failed, God would reach down for them and draw them up to paradise.

Bolan worked his way southward, through the dripping woods, hidden by tangled weeds and brush. In three minutes he was directly above the Shiites, a few yards up the bank, at the edge of the woods.

These men were less formally dressed than the one who had dumped the garbage—they wore tattered jackets over stained white T-shirts. The Shiites peered casually around the clearing, focusing their attention mainly up the road, from which they obviously expected someone to come. And all the while they conversed quietly in a language totally incomprehensible to Mack Bolan.

The warrior crawled closer, until only a shield of heavy green weeds concealed him from view, and lay watching. One of the Shiites began to speak more loudly, more firmly. The other nodded and laughed. Then the first man drew a knife from his belt. His intention was obvious—he was going to slash the tires on the BMW.

Bolan grabbed at a bit of fallen branch that lay beside him and threw it onto the road beyond the car, where it landed with a clatter.

The burp guns whirled around. The men didn't fire, but they leveled their weapons and trotted forward, probing the shadows. While their attention was diverted, Bolan picked up a midsize rock, and threw it onto the road behind them. They swung around, still disciplined about firing, but jerking the muzzles from side to side, ready to loose a deadly burst at anything that moved. Bolan hugged the wet ground and watched.

The men were alert and frightened, and stood away from the BMW, as if it were alive. They conversed for a long moment, then one of them strode up the road toward the gate and the house, going for reinforcements. The other faced the car, raising and lowering his burp gun, trying to decide if he should fire a quick burst to disable it.

Bolan couldn't allow that. He drew the sound-suppressed Lahti and took careful aim. For a moment the Shiite seemed indecisive, then he raised his weapon toward the nose of the BMW. Bolan fired first. The 9 mm slug from the Finnish pistol struck the man in the middle of the chest, and he collapsed in a heap near the vehicle.

The other Iranian had rounded the curve in the lane and was out of sight. Bolan raced down to the BMW, unlocked it and slid behind the wheel. The engine caught on the first try. The other Shiite heard the noise and hustled back. Bolan jammed the vehicle into gear, gunned the engine and sped forward. The Shiite instinctively raised the muzzle of his gun, but he was too slow. The nose of the BMW struck him hard and he fell back on the gravel, the front wheels passing over him.

Bolan stopped the vehicle, got out and hurried over to the struggling man, whose legs were broken. He saw Bolan and tried to lift his gun to get off a burst. Bolan was ready with the Lahti. The bullet tore through the man's throat.

He couldn't leave the bodies behind; he heaved them into the trunk of the car. The men in the house might think they'd been picked up by the guy in the Renault—or perhaps that they'd had enough and had defected. He drove south, high into the Massif. On a remote road he stopped and dumped the bodies into a weed-choked ditch. He changed into his tourist clothes and cleaned his face of the green combat cosmetics.

He left the Czech-manufactured submachine guns with the bodies. The weapons had only one clip in each, so they wouldn't have added much to his arsenal. Anyway, when the French found them, they'd know the Shiites for what they were by the weapons they had carried.

13

The *Santa Margherita* rounded the Môle and entered the *ancien bassin*, the older, bigger yacht basin at Saint-Tropez, shortly past noon. Expertly piloted, the big, black-hulled yacht backed into its reserved space at the quay. As always, the magnificent vessel was the focus of attention for the hundreds of tourists who strolled the quay at that time of day.

This afternoon the padrone, who ordinarily enjoyed the admiring stares of tourists, could have done without so much attention. He'd brought armed reinforcements to defend the laboratory against an anticipated attack, and he would have liked to see his men slip off the boat unnoticed. If Bolan was working against him, then who else? Were there French police agents in that tourist crowd? His men didn't possess a look of innocence and couldn't mime it. He wished there was some way to unload his reinforcements without anyone observing.

FROM HIS ROOM at the Byblos Hotel, Mack Bolan watched the yacht through his binoculars and saw the hardmen leaving the yacht one by one. Soldiers. The padrone was bringing in Corsicans to reinforce his security at the laboratory. He knew about the penetration of lab security the previous night, and he was beefing it up with tough Corsican gunmen.

Then Bolan spotted something more interesting. The maroon Renault was parked on the quay.

He hadn't seen the driver board the *Santa Margherita*, but he had no doubt the driver was aboard. Vittorio Muro was stirred to anger and to action, and no doubt he had summoned the man in the Renault by a dawn radiotelephone call, which would explain why the Renault had rushed down the lane just before Bolan encountered the men waiting by his BMW. The master had called.

On the other hand, that didn't explain why the man had been summoned so early, when the yacht wouldn't reach the port before noon. What had the driver of the Renault been up to all morning? Another interesting question.

What Bolan *didn't* see was Emily. Where was she? He was determined to find out, even if he had to somehow board the yacht. He *would* find out. Whatever it cost.

EMILY WAS ASLEEP in her cabin. She'd been up most of the night, and there was nothing she could do now. Muro had not summoned her to lunch. She couldn't leave the boat without his permission, and he had suggested to her that he'd put her ashore once they docked at Saint-Tropez. She saw no reason to suppose he wouldn't.

EMILY HADN'T BEEN SUMMONED to lunch because Muro and his sister-in-law were holding a council in the main lounge. Andres Kostenjevac, the man who drove the maroon Renault, was with them.

They spoke Italian, Kostenjevac with an accent that made him difficult to understand. "I rented the vans. Your men have left for Barjols in them. Also, I took care of the matter of Thuret."

"I assumed you would," Muro replied coldly, "since those were my orders. I'm concerned about something else. I've had a call from the laboratory. Two of the Iranians are missing. Michel wanted to know if you had brought them with you. Did you? If not, what explanation do you have?"

"They are missing?" Kostenjevac asked, frowning hard. "You mean . . . ?"

"The word *missing* is simple enough, isn't it? They have disappeared," Muro said. "They went out to check around the premises last night, after your alarm system went off, and they have not returned."

"The alarm . . ." Kostenjevac shrugged. "In a storm like that, it was nothing but a limb falling on one of the sensors in the woods. It has happened before."

"Ah, so," Muro replied wryly. "And a window was broken in the laboratory."

"Signor," Kostenjevac said. "You have rarely seen such a storm. Anyway, nothing happened—"

"Except that two men disappeared," Giovanna Sestri interrupted. "How do you explain that?"

Kostenjevac shrugged again. "Iranians. You can't depend on them. They're probably off praying somewhere. Praying or... Well, you can't ever be sure. They are moved by strange, irrational impulses."

"I suggest we do not assume they are off praying or anything of the kind," Muro said. "Assumptions like that can be very dangerous. Anyway, they have not returned, and a good many hours have passed. You say nothing happened last night. I say two of your Iranians were either killed or taken into custody. In either case—"

"We are under attack," Giovanna finished, "by the most dangerous man in the world."

"Bolan, you mean," Kostenjevac concluded. "That, too, is an assumption. Indeed, do we actually know that such a man as this Mack Bolan really exists? Is it not possible that this man is a myth, perhaps one invented by frightened men trying to set up a rationalization for their own failures, their own mistakes?"

"When his only victims were assorted American street thugs, I thought so," Muro replied. "When he appeared in Europe and some of his victims were intelligent businessmen, I changed my mind. He is real, Kostenjevac. You can be sure of it."

"But no one even knows what he looks like," Kostenjevac protested. "A phantom... Why, he could be aboard this boat. He could be one of your crew."

"Use your brains, Andres," Giovanna snapped. "Assuming you have any. He killed Dicomano while the *Santa Margherita* was at sea."

"And right under your nose, sister-in-law," Muro taunted. "Right under that sharply uplifted nose of yours, my self-righteous kinswoman."

"The man you sent to protect me did nothing," she complained. "An incompetent. I am fortunate it was Dicomano that Bolan elected to murder."

Muro shrugged. Abruptly, almost irrationally, his mood changed. "In all my years as a businessman, I have never become involved in an enterprise with such potential for profit as this one."

"Nor an enterprise more fraught with hazard," Giovanna added.

"Nor one more fraught with hazard," Muro agreed. "But think! With the profit from this traffic, we will be able to buy anything we want. Presidents, prime ministers, generals. Whole nations!"

"If we are not destroyed by Mack Bolan first," his sister-in-law muttered.

"The key," Muro said, "is the woman."

"What woman?" Kostenjevac asked.

"He is said to be accompanied by a woman, an American intelligence agent. Bolan leads a charmed life. Maybe she doesn't. If we could find her—"

"My brother-in-law," Giovanna said scornfully, "is satisfied that the American girl who just happened to charm him by her singing on the quay, and whom he invited aboard the yacht, is not this American agent—this in spite of the fact that she charmed her way on board and has been here during these past few troubling days."

"I tell you, she could not—"

"Maybe not. But she could have been sending messages? Are you absolutely certain she hasn't? What if she is in radio contact with Bolan? What if she has some means of signaling. What then, Vittorio?"

Muro smiled. "She came aboard nearly naked. And she has remained so, except when I dressed her to spare the sensibilities of some of the family at the villa. Where do you suppose she carries this radio?"

"In her guitar, of course," Giovanna replied. "Or in the case. How closely have you examined them? A miniature radio is easily enough concealed in a musical instrument."

Vittorio Muro flushed. He glared at his sister-in-law. "Very well. Let's settle the matter. I will examine her guitar and case. Then I will pay her off and put her ashore. And if our troubles end when she is gone, so much the better. You may believe she was the cause. I will not."

The three of them sipped red wine while a crewman went below to waken Emily and summon her to the lounge. She was told to bring her guitar and the case, as well as anything else that was hers. She was going ashore.

EMILY WAS ANXIOUS to leave the yacht. She had a lot to report to Bolan. They had said that the laboratory was near Barjols. Knowing that, how difficult could it be to find? It was the information they most needed, and she knew the importance of relaying that intel as soon as possible.

She entered the lounge, wearing the clothes she'd worn on the quay the day Muro had noticed her. The woman with him—whoever she was—was more grim, more disapproving, than the sour-faced one at the villa who had called her a whore. The second man in the lounge was curious and skeptical, but appreciative just the same. His stare was a leer.

"Linda," Muro said. "Sit down. Have a glass of wine. We are about to say farewell to you. Reluctantly. As I told you, business will require my strict attention for some time, and I am afraid I will not be able to claim your time any longer."

"I will be sorry to leave, *signor*."

"I am sorry to part with you. Your singing and playing have been a comfort."

"Thank you, but I'm strictly an amateur," she replied.

"You speak fluent Italian," Giovanna Sestri observed. "How many Texans—"

"Many can speak it, *signora*," Emily told her. "It's not so different from Spanish, after all, and many Texans are of Spanish ancestry."

"I have never played a musical instrument," Giovanna said. "I always wished to." She reached for the guitar. "Do you mind? I do enjoy plucking the strings."

Emily wasn't deceived. The woman was lying. She wanted to examine the guitar. There was no point in saying something foolish, such as that a musical instrument is a highly personal possession. She could only watch the grim woman take the guitar from its case and begin to examine it.

Muro allowed an amused smile to spread across his face. "Are you satisfied, sister-in-law?"

"Yes, I am quite satisfied," Giovanna replied. "It is as I suspected. See here. An electronic device inside. I shall now send a message to Signor Bolan—"

"No!" Emily shrieked as the woman pushed the handle of a fork into the guitar and pressed a switch on the tiny transmitter mounted inside.

The radio signal reached the detonator in a fraction of an instant. The explosion, in the stern of the yacht and deep inside its hull, was only a muffled thump. But a moment later smoke and fire erupted from the stern as burning oil spilled from the ruptured tank where last night Emily had attached the little package of plastique.

Emily jumped to her feet and ran for the upper deck. Muro yelled orders while Giovanna Sestri screamed. Emily ran for the rail, intending to jump overboard, to swim away from the *Santa Margherita* and the padrone. A shot was fired. She didn't know if someone was shooting at her or—

It made no difference. A crewman, heeding the furiously shouted orders of Muro, had grabbed her arm and held her so tightly that she couldn't break loose before another crewman emphatically leveled the muzzle of a Luger on her.

"So!" Muro barked. "My sister-in-law was right. We need not jump into the water, my child. We can walk down the gangplank to my car. And we will go where we can ask the questions and receive the answers that will untangle this mystery."

Chaos. The crew ran onto the decks, milling about in confusion. An alarm bell clanged; the Saint-Tropez fire horn began to screech. Crewmen on the adjacent yachts threw lines overboard as they struggled to push their own boats away from the quay and the fiercely burning *Santa Margherita*. The second fuel tank exploded, blowing a hole in the hull and throwing fire out over the water. Oily black smoke spread throughout the yacht. The grim woman who had triggered the explosion staggered out of the rear cabin, coughing and cursing.

Emily was at the center of a small, struggling knot of men who shouldered their way down the gangplank, forcing a way for the padrone, his sister-in-law and their prisoner. The driver of Muro's car had the engine running. A bodyguard opened the doors. Emily was thrown into the back seat and shoved facedown onto the floor. The car laid rubber as it left the quay.

SIRENS BLARING across the waterfront drew Bolan's attention. He grabbed the binoculars and ran out on the balcony where he could scan the scene on the quay. The *Santa Margherita* was afire, burning fiercely, and already beginning to settle, stern first. Whether Emily was aboard was impossible to say. The scene on the quay was one of utter confusion. Firefighters had difficulty pressing through the milling crowd that grew larger every second. People were running both toward the fire and away from it. Who was running where was impossible to tell. Bolan jammed the Lahti into his harness and bolted for the door.

Yvette rushed into his room. She had abandoned a modeling assignment and hurried to join him. They rushed out of the room and down to the garage.

"No more incognito!" she shouted. "We go as investigators. Police Judiciare."

Bolan nodded his agreement. He drove the BMW as near as he could to the dock. Yvette stuck a police identification card on the dashboard, and they left it parked on a sidewalk and pushed their way through the crowd toward the burning yacht.

"Police Judiciare!" Yvette cried as she ran up to a uniformed policeman. *"Monsieur, je suis Inspecteur Duclos."* She showed her identity card. *"C'affaire ci c'est une affaire de la sécurité nationale!"*

The policeman, as dumbfounded as any of his kind would be in the face of what he heard from this extraordinary woman, acceded to the demand that he open a way for them to the stern of the sinking yacht.

As Bolan watched, the stern of the *Santa Margherita* settled under the water. Water and debris gushed over the deck and poured down the gangway into the already flooding interior. The yacht sank fast then, its mooring lines snapping. When the entire length of the keel was imbedded in the slime at the bottom of the basin, the *Santa Margherita* listed thirty degrees to port, and more water poured over the rail and into its hull. The fire went out, mostly, except for flames on the oil that floated on the surface. Firemen shot foam over that, and in a minute or two the fire was out entirely, and the last of the heavy black smoke drifted away.

The yacht seemed to shudder, then heeled over on its side. The heavy masts crashed down on a big motor yacht, crushing that boat's superstructure and breaking through its main cabin to the level of the deck. Its spars crashed through the deck and penetrated the motor yacht's hull under water. The vessel began to sink as its owner screamed and cursed on the quay.

Yvette questioned the uniformed policeman. Yes, the people aboard the yacht had gotten off. No, he didn't think anyone had been killed. Where had they gone? The policeman heaved a Gallic shrug and threw out his hands. All around. They could by anywhere. Had anyone from the yacht left in a car? Oh, yes. Two cars had pushed their way out of the crowd. He pointed eastward.

Much of their French was too fast and idiomatic for Bolan, but he had caught the mention of two cars. He grabbed the officer's arm. *"Un Renault marron?"* he demanded.

"Oui, monsieur. Et un Mercedes bleu."

"Helicopter!" Bolan snapped at Yvette. "We need that helicopter!"

They used the officer's radio to relay the call. They shouldered their way out of the crowd and trotted toward the Saint-Tropez heliport, which was just beyond the smaller yacht basin. They reached the landing pad in less than ten minutes, and the police chopper was already in sight. In five more minutes they were in the air.

"Barjols!" Bolan yelled to the pilot. "We want a maroon Renault and a blue Mercedes. Take 558, then west on the Autoroute and north along 554."

They spotted the two cars on the Autoroute. Bolan told the pilot to stay high, to follow without being seen. The Renault led the way, followed by the Mercedes. Both vehicles turned off at Brignoles, followed Route N554 north, passed through the village of Barjols and turned onto the country road that led to the laboratory-factory.

"Muro," Bolan muttered. "And Emily."

"You can't be sure," Yvette replied.

"Of Emily? No. And we can't go down for a look-see when they reach the laboratory. If they spot a chopper overhead, who knows what they'll do?"

"If she is alive, Mack—"

"She's with them, and she makes a perfect hostage."

"And what's your government's official policy about that?" Yvette asked. "What sacrifices are you supposed to make to free hostages?"

"I don't work for any government. I make my own rules."

"NOT IN FRANCE, you don't," Inspector Grimmaud stated bluntly. "We have rules, too. Very firm ones. And we have operated very effectively within them. I cannot permit you to go out on a one-man operation."

They stood on the heliport in the bright low sun of late afternoon. Besides Grimmaud, a high-ranking uniformed police officer was there, as well as an army officer in sunglasses, kepi and khaki summer uniform.

"'Permit,'" Bolan repeated. "Am I under arrest? Do you mean to restrain me?"

"No, of course not," Grimmaud replied, exasperated. "On the other hand, we did supply you with arms, which are technically in your possession illegally. I am afraid I shall have to trouble you for their return."

"I'm afraid you'll have to find them," Bolan growled. "I lost them last night."

The warrior had, in fact, anticipated something like this, so this morning, after he returned and before he went to his room for some sleep, he'd rented another car—a tiny white Simca, with a four-banger engine that sounded about powerful enough to run a medium-size lawn mower. It was parked on a hillside street a short distance from the Byblos Hotel. His Luger and the Beretta submachine gun were hidden in the little car. He carried the Lahti. They would take that if they searched him.

"I understand you," Grimmaud said, "and I know what motivates you. But please believe me, Bolan. Please . . . You can't improve on our methods. We will rescue Miss Grant and close down the laboratory."

"How?" Bolan asked bluntly.

Grimmaud glanced into the face of Yvette Duclos. "We will combine two effective methods. First, we will surround the laboratory with an armed force so great they cannot hope to engage us in a firefight. Then we will negotiate the release of your woman agent."

"How soon?" Bolan asked. "Would you mind telling me your plan?"

"It will take a little time to assemble the force," Grimmaud replied. "We have been talking, Major Ambert and I. We are thinking of surrounding the laboratory just before dawn, then making a show of force at dawn. There will be armored vehicles, armed helicopters, rocket launchers, five hundred men from the Special Operations Force. We—"

"You assume they'll wait all night for you to assemble your force," Bolan said. "What makes you think Muro will still be there? Isn't it more likely he'll anticipate something like what you're planning and make his escape before your show of force is possible?"

"We have already begun to surround the place. The roads are covered now."

"Vittorio Muro is not the kind of man to allow himself to be trapped like a rat in a sewer," Bolan said. "Don't underestimate him, Grimmaud. He has resources we hardly know of. What's more, he has no interest whatsoever in making a heroic stand. If he feels threatened, if he sees the least possibility of being taken, he'll get out of there."

"If he is in fact there now, he will remain there," Grimmaud said firmly. "We are shutting him in."

"And what am I expected to do?"

"I pray of you, Bolan, to stay with us. When Major Ambert and I go to Barjols to assume command, you are welcome to accompany us. When we negotiate—*if* we negotiate—you can take the most active role. If there is an assault, you can go in the lead if you wish. But please, until we can work cooperatively, do not try anything on your own. I will not subject you to any indignity, such as arrest. I respect you too much for that. I rely on your intelligence and good judgment."

"Thank you, Inspector," Bolan replied dryly. "I'll use both of them."

As Bolan walked away, back toward the quay where he had abandoned the BMW, Grimmaud turned to Yvette. "Your assignment, Inspector Duclos, is to stay with that man. Report what he does. If he makes an attempt to go to Barjols on his own, we will have to stop him."

"It won't be easy," she said.

"It would be more difficult still if I had told him another bit of news. There was a triple murder aboard the *Mistral* this morning. Thuret, an employee and—"

"The daughter?"

Grimmaud nodded. "Brigitte Thuret, nineteen years old."

"Have you any suspects?"

"No. It was professionally done. A grim massacre. To silence Thuret, one must suppose. How would Bolan react if he knew that?"

"Don't underestimate Mack Bolan, Inspector," Yvette warned. "He would not go wild. He would just become more deadly."

"Don't let him get away from you," Grimmaud ordered. He looked after Bolan, who was striding rapidly toward the quay. "We have installed a radio beeper in one of the fenders of the BMW, but I would rather you maintain personal contact."

14

Yvette caught up with Bolan as he hurried toward the BMW. He knew why she had followed. She was a striking and erotic woman, but she was also an agent of the Police Judiciare, and she would do her duty. He drove her back to the hotel, and he went to his room, telling her he had to change his clothes before he could go down to dinner with her. Her behavior was predictable. She waited in the hall, a few doors away from his room, where she could see if he came out.

He took his time. Let her wait a while. Let her grow impatient. For him to get away from her without doing something to her, she had to make a mistake. The more burdensome she found her assignment, the more likely she would be to make one. Impatience was the source of many errors.

When Bolan was ready, he opened the door. "Oh," he said. "What a coincidence. I was just coming to *your* room. Are you ready for dinner?"

Yvette smiled at the irony she heard in his voice. "If you don't mind," she replied a little coldly, "I'd like to use your bathroom before we go down to dinner."

He stood aside as she hurried through his bedroom and into the bathroom. She went inside and locked the door. Why? he wondered. To check her pistol? To take out a sleeping pill that she would slip in his wine at the dinner table?

It made no difference. He moved a heavy chair to the bathroom door, wedged it securely under the knob and left the room. Yvette was resourceful, and she'd be out in a few minutes—even if she had to use her pistol to draw attention to her plight. But by then he'd be long gone. He regretted having to do that to her. She was a superior kind of young woman; but he had a job to do.

Bolan hurried down the stairs, out past the pool and through the lobby to the parking garage. Fortunately, the BMW was still there. When he drove out of the garage, Yvette hadn't yet raised an alarm.

He drove the vehicle away from the hotel, toward the village square where in the evening the old men played at *boules*. He parked it there, in the first spot he could find. The PJ wouldn't find it for a while, and until they did they'd be searching for the BMW, not the little Simca. He trotted back up, unlocked the white Simca, checked his cache of weapons and drove away toward Barjols.

Bolan drove along the coast to Sainte-Maxime, then north to Le Muy and Draguignan, then west over a twisting mountain road to Salernes. He was approaching from the east this time, and he didn't have to enter the village of Barjols at all. Instead he took Route D32 direct to the intersection with the road to the laboratory. The French forces converging on the lab would probably set up headquarters in Barjols; Grimmaud himself might be there by now. By avoiding Barjols he might at least avoid a confrontation with the Inspector.

The French forces—police and military—*were* converging. There was no question of that. On the road in the last red light of sunset before the sky turned black and starry, Bolan saw a dozen police vans and a score of army trucks. They were assembling nothing less than an army for an assault on the padrone's laboratory.

Grimmaud had spoken of road blocks. If he expected Bolan to approach the laboratory only by road, he shouldn't have consented to his flying in the helicopter that followed the Renault and the Mercedes that afternoon. Bolan had taken the time as the chopper circled high above the villa to scout the lay of the land. He knew how to evade whatever roadblocks the French might have in place. He knew a better way to enter the laboratory compound.

The previous night he'd gone directly up the lane, then through the woods and had blundered into the sensors planted throughout the woods. He wouldn't risk that way again.

The cluster of buildings was surrounded by woods and was also encircled by an electric fence. The sensors formed another circle, no doubt. A mountain stream ran through the woods to the east. Another country road, to the west, ran north and south.

If there were twenty armed men on the premises the night before, there were probably double that number now. Most of the security men he'd seen previously were

Iranians. But the heavies who had left the *Santa Margherita* immediately after she docked were no Middle Easterners; they were menacing enforcers from Union Corse. If one of them found a Shiite half-asleep at the gatehouse tonight, he'd slit the man's throat. Those hardcases didn't believe God would help them win their battles—they believed in winning by being tougher and more cruel than their enemies could ever imagine.

One thing, though—if Vittorio Muro was inside the compound, there was more than one way out. He wouldn't allow himself to be trapped, wouldn't have gone to the lab this afternoon if he'd supposed he could be backed into a corner by French police. He wouldn't place himself inside a circle from which there was no escape. He had another way out. Bolan was sure of it. And whatever was Vittorio Muro's way out was Mack Bolan's way in.

He'd thought about that while the helicopter hovered far above. He didn't see a helipad on the hill. Which made sense. Escape by air wasn't an effective way of getting away. A chopper couldn't lift off without a clatter, and once in the air it would become a blip on air-traffic-control radar. Pursuit and interception would be relatively easy.

No, there had to be another way in and out of the compound. Perhaps there was a tunnel or perhaps something simple, like a secret path through the sensors. Or maybe something more clever, something the padrone was confident no one would ever guess.

But what good would a tunnel or a path do if it didn't lead to a more rapid means of escape from the area? As Bolan analyzed it, somewhere there had to be a carefully hidden vehicle—or vehicles. The top dogs in the compound would let the foot soldiers die defending the place, and maybe the heavies, too, while they slipped out along some escape route that the others didn't know about. The padrones of Union Corse hadn't dominated their special world for so many years by making concessions to their serfs.

Finally, he guessed Muro would bring Emily out with him. She was his hostage, his bargaining chip. By now the padrone would know he had Bolan to contend with—Bolan, the Executioner. If there was a confrontation, she would be Vittorio Muro's play—her life for his escape.

Bolan avoided the French roadblocks by parking the Simca beside a road about two miles from the compound. There he changed into his camouflage fatigues and painted his face. He hung the Lahti on one hip in a snapped-shut holster and tucked the Luger into one of the deep pockets of the fatigues.

The Beretta submachine gun wasn't equipped with a shoulder sling and was awkward to carry. He had no choice but to cradle it under his arm. He carried his extra ammunition and magazines stuffed in a black canvas knapsack he could strap over his shoulders. After a final weapons check, Bolan was up and running with only two goals in mind: find Emily Grant, and destroy the heroin factory. Taking out Vittorio Muro would be a bonus.

YVETTE WAS both angry and embarrassed when she finally managed to escape from the bathroom. As Bolan had anticipated, she finally had to fire her Beretta out the bathroom window, which effectively blew her cover. Yvette was no longer a tall, dramatically made-up fashion model; she was an armed police agent, sharply demanding, snapping out orders.

She went to her room and put through her call to headquarters: find the BMW by tracking the radio beepers placed in its fenders. But stay away from the vehicle. She would be the one to apprehend Bolan.

Twenty minutes later, dressed now in tight blue-denim jeans and a black nylon jacket that inadequately covered her shoulder holster, Yvette stood and stared at the abandoned BMW. Gone now was the .22 pocket Beretta she had fired from Bolan's bathroom window. She'd replaced that weapon with a Beretta Model 12, the same submachine gun PJ had issued to Bolan.

The beepers the technicians had planted in the BMW still forlornly signaled its location to PJ receivers in cars around the square. Damn! Bolan was clever. Too damned clever by half. Clever enough to get himself killed, and Emily Grant, as well. Clever enough to ruin tonight's operation.

Grimmaud had gone to Barjols. Yvette demanded a helicopter and set out on a night flight to join him. She had no doubt Bolan was somewhere in that neighborhood.

BOLAN HAD CROSSED some fields of mustard and a vineyard, and had circled around a field of ripening wheat so he wouldn't break it down and leave a trail. The wooded hill, where the lab was located, loomed ahead.

As he crossed a narrow meadow, a helicopter passed overhead, lights blazing. The French weren't being particularly subtle by flying a noisy helicopter overhead. They were surrounding Muro with a growing ring of armed force. Still, unless Muro was the fool Bolan knew he was not, Muro had a way out. The point was to find it.

He came to the little stream he'd seen from the air. That put him a quarter of a mile or so downhill from the eastern edge of the compound. He waded across the peaceful, tumbling mountain stream in the dim light of a yellow moon that had risen a few minutes ago. Then he climbed the steep, muddy bank to the edge of the woods beyond.

An escape route had to bring Muro to a road. The country road to the south of the compound was blocked for sure. The road to the west... Police or soldiers would have blocked that, too.

What about a vehicle that didn't need a road? A possibility. Some kind of all-terrain vehicle. A small tank? Could Muro and his gang actually have a tank? It wasn't impossible. Muro had money enough to buy a battalion of tanks if he wanted them. After all, it was Muro's money that had bought a Foxbat for the attempt on the life of the President of the United States.

Whatever means of escape Muro had, it had to be found at the end of a path through the compound's security. Bolan had seen the south approach to the compound. He began to circle to the north, through the woods to the east, working his way around the perimeter of the hill.

He didn't try to get closer to the compound—he knew where it was, and there was no point in risking an alarm. In any case, it was unlikely that the escape vehicle was close to the compound. More likely it would be found a few hundred yards outside the perimeter fence, far enough away to remain undiscovered by attackers converging on the compound.

The hill rose above him, rocky and wooded. The compound sat on the summit. From the wooded slope, looking back in the moonlight, he could see the little mountain stream splashing along. Beyond it lay the fields, and beyond the fields were small farmhouses showing placid yellowish light in their windows.

Bolan made his way up the hill, intending to go high enough to be able to look down into the compound. He ventured as close as he dared, not wanting to risk entering the field of sensors, and climbed a tree.

From halfway up he could make out the compound through the woods. Lights were blazing. As many as a dozen Iranians patrolled the perimeter, stalking menacingly around the lawn, weapons up and ready. Sure. The padrone was in residence, and the guards would have been out no matter what the weather, no matter what the hour. Security was tight; nerves were tighter. Which could be worse. Or better—tension was the forefather of mistakes, just like impatience.

Four vans, lined up on the far side of the house, were being worked on by three hardmen. They were installing something in the back of one of them. If the warrior guessed correctly, they were filling the vehicle with explosives, creating an option for themselves: hit one of the roadblocks with a huge blast and rush through with the rest of the vehicles—including, of course, the Renault and Mercedes—before the dust settled.

That would be a desperate move, and he didn't think Muro would take that risk. He would be going out another way. With Emily.

If he hadn't already.

A thundering, fiery explosion suddenly tore the laboratory apart. In an instant the whole building had vanished, debris rattling down on the roof of the house, where the explosion had shattered all the windows on the east side. As the smoke blew away, nothing was left of the lab but the foundation and a heap of smoldering rubble. The leaders of the alliance had destroyed as much evidence as they could.

Surely the French would move in now, and surely Muro would move out. Bolan dropped from the tree. Staying clear of the sensors was no longer important. Muro and his confederates knew they were surrounded and were preparing to break out. Or to fight. He trotted toward the fence.

The angry, harsh roar of weapons fire almost deafened Bolan as the slugs tore into the trunk of a tree just behind him. He threw himself to the ground, rolling as he hit the dirt. Another burst tore into the earth where he'd been standing a second earlier.

The gunfire came from inside the compound, through the fence. He spotted the man, who was one of the Corsican hardmen. The gunner stood up boldly, searching the woods for another sight of the man he had fired on. Several men raced across the compound to join him. Bolan leveled the Beretta and loosed a quick burst. The hardman fell, but the others kept coming, firing as they ran toward the fence, shattering the woods with a storm of indiscriminate fire.

From somewhere in the woods someone yelled a sharp command in Italian. Bolan rolled over and peered into the moonlit woods. And he saw Muro and Emily! She was almost naked, wearing nothing but a skimpy white bikini, and her hands were tied behind her.

Muro kept a tight grip on her arm, pushing her forward at a fast pace down the hill. Another man followed. He carried a weapon Bolan recognized even at this distance by its unmistakable profile—an Uzi, one of those with two magazines welded together at right angles so that one extended forward under the barrel and was instantly available to reload the weapon. The three kept so close together that Bolan didn't dare to fire.

What was worse, he couldn't get up to follow them. He was pinned down by the panicky, uneven fire from the Iranians in the compound.

He rolled back to face the fence, to see what chance he had to drop all of the opposition. They were spread out, yelling and firing, calling for reinforcements. Bolan rose to a crouch and let go with everything that was left in his magazine. Two men went down and stayed down. Another jumped around screaming, trying to stem the flow of blood from a leg wound.

As Bolan grabbed another magazine from his sack and rammed it into the Beretta, the wounded Iranian steadied himself on his good leg and fired into the woods. Several men joined him, knelt and opened fire. For whatever reason—wild fanaticism, blind faith—they were brave. They had Bolan trapped so that he couldn't pursue Muro.

Bolan put the Beretta aside and pulled the Finnish pistol from its holster. He knew it was exceptionally accurate, and besides, the sound suppressor would make it more difficult for the Iranians to figure out his exact position.

Lying prone, with some of their wild fire cutting the air above him, Bolan extended the Lahti in both hands, aimed and squeezed off a shot. An Iranian shrieked, dropped his Czech subgun and fell to the ground. Bolan shot again and took out the man with the leg wound. The lone survivor ceased firing and turned to run toward the rubble of the laboratory, yelling wildly for help.

Bolan crawled backward until he was out of sight of the compound. Then he crouch-walked as quietly as he could down the hill.

Muro had a substantial lead, but Bolan couldn't risk blundering into him. If the man with the Uzi was calm and steady, he would drop anyone who came near. And Muro had Emily at his mercy.

Before the warrior could pick up the trail, the French forces broke into action. They had brought floodlights, which now blazed over the crest of the hill behind him, illuminating the entire southern slope of the hill. He could hear engines grinding, which indicated the French bringing up equipment. One of their choppers hovered overhead. Every road would be blocked now. The forces would be spreading out, forming their skirmish lines, covering every approach to the hill.

Bolan reached the stream where it was at its deepest, and plunged across, wetting himself to the waist. On the other side he trotted out of the woods and onto the little meadow he had crossed earlier.

A buzzing drew the warrior's attention and he threw himself on his face and rolled out of the way as an airplane rose off the ground only a few yards away.

He turned and stared up at the plane, which resembled a huge bat. It turned to the east, and as it passed between him and the moon he saw what it was—a Fieseler Storch, an old German scout plane, the kind Otto Skorzeny had landed on an Italian mountaintop in 1944 when he rescued Mussolini; the kind Rommel had flown in Africa. It was called a Stork because of the long struts of its landing gear, designed to let it take off and land on very rough ground. It was hugely overpowered by a single inverted V-6 engine, which could lift it into the air without strain, without a telltale roar, with less than a hundred-foot run. Its high wings were oversized and slotted for lift, and they could be folded back so the planes could be more easily hidden.

He had heard that a few of them still flew, preserved as sport planes by aviation buffs. This one was painted black. It had climbed only a few hundred feet above the ground and was now speeding away at more than a hundred miles an hour, all but invisible both from the ground and from the air. Flying low, it could sneak under French radar. And it could land almost anywhere a helicopter could land.

Vittorio Muro had escaped, and Emily was with him.

For a moment Bolan stood watching the elusive silhouette of the Storch as it blended into the dark night sky and disappeared. Angry and frustrated, he clenched and unclenched his fists.

The sound of gunfire on the hill above him captured his attention. He turned toward the hill and the sounds of battle. He had a job to do here. Vittorio Muro was now out of reach.

Bolan knelt on the damp earth and took a moment to reload his magazines.

Bolan knelt on the damp earth and took a moment to reload his magazines.

15

The French obviously didn't know that Vittorio Muro had escaped. They continued to develop their plan. They would surround the compound, show their force and open talks. The explosion inside the compound hadn't moved them to choose another course of action. Neither had the firefight on the eastern slope of the hill. They were tightening the ring, with dull military precision—soldiers and policemen unimaginatively doing what soldiers and policemen knew how to do. Bolan could see and hear their slow, cautious approach. They would move in at dawn, as Grimmaud had said. That was what they had planned, and that was what they were going to do.

While the French delayed, the hardmen inside the compound were busy preparing nasty surprises for them—explosives, especially.

They had already blown up the laboratory. Not that the French were going to worry much about the destruction of evidence. They didn't worry as much about evidence as American police did. They had ways of dealing with crime that would shock the toughest New York street cop, much less an American judge. In the old days Action Service had simply eliminated anyone identified as a dangerous enemy of the state. Today, though the government of France would deny it, GIGN had inherited that function.

None of which did a damned bit of good if Muro had escaped.

The French had another surprise coming—a breakout, effected by ramming one of their roadblocks with a van loaded with enough explosives to scatter policemen and soldiers over half of southern France, followed by a rush through the gap. That was what Bolan had seen the hardmen preparing in the compound.

These guys were tough, some of them fanatics, the rest experienced professional enforcers for a criminal combine that made the Costa Nostra look like sandbox kids.

Bolan wondered if Grimmaud understood that. Surely he did—the man was no fool. But Grimmaud was methodical, plodding, careful. And maybe he wasn't in command. This had developed into a big operation, perhaps too big for a police inspector. It was possible that the military was in command.

Bolan reached the perimeter again, from where he could see into the compound. Someone had turned off the lights, but he could see the Corsicans and Iranians still working, running in and out of the house, carrying something to the vans. What? he wondered. Heroin, maybe. If they were going to risk their lives they wouldn't leave millions of dollars' worth of the stuff behind.

The men he'd shot a few minutes earlier still lay on the ground just inside the fence. Nobody had bothered to come out and drag them away. He walked up to the fence. His problem right now was that the fence was almost certainly still electrified, with high voltage. He couldn't take the chance of touching to find out. He trotted along it, moving south, toward the southeast corner of the compound. The fence was close to the treeline in some places, and maybe he could climb a tree, work his way out on a limb and drop on the other side of the fence.

A rustling sound in the underbrush told the warrior that something—or someone—was behind him. He dropped to his knees and brought up the muzzle of the Beretta.

Whatever it was, it was cautious. It moved, then stopped to listen, then moved again, approaching the fence very slowly. Bolan caught sight of a human silhouette in the cold white moonlight—a black jacket; a tall, thin...

"Yvette?"

"Mack?"

She was dressed in tight blue-denim jeans, a black nylon jacket and thick-soled hiking boots. She carried a Beretta Model 12 submachine gun, the same as his own. Bolan could tell that the woman wore a shoulder holster. The lumpy nylon bag she toted was filled, he supposed, with extra magazines of ammunition.

"Why couldn't you have waited?" she whispered. "I knew it had to be you up here. I was afraid you had been killed. Why—"

"Muro has already left," Bolan cut in. "Five minutes ago. He had Emily with him."

"If we had moved faster..." she sighed.

"It wouldn't have made any difference. Muro would have taken off as soon as he saw you were getting close. If you could have gotten here in daylight, we'd have had a better chance. But—"

"How?" she asked. "How did he get away? The roads... They're all covered."

"He flew," Bolan replied. "He had an airplane hidden down there in the fields somewhere, probably in a barn. And they've blown up the lab."

"Then maybe they're going to try to break out," she said. "That's what they'll do, won't they? But our people are ready. The roads are blocked."

"How?"

"We've parked cars and vans across them. And we've blanketed the area with armed men. They won't get through."

"They'll get through, "Bolan said grimly. "They're going to ram one of your roadblocks with a vanload of explosives. Are your people ready for anything like that?"

Yvette shook her head. "I don't know."

"You'd better go back with a warning. I'm going to try to—"

"I can't go back," she said. "I had a helicopter drop me in the field below the hill, and the pilot returned to the command post in Barjols. I don't know where the nearest police or army unit is. How much time do we have?"

Bolan looked toward the compound. "Not much. I'd say a matter of minutes."

"What can we do?" she asked.

"Shoot the hell out of the place," he said. "But that fence is charged with a whole lot of volts."

"I can take care of that." Yvette jammed her hand into the shoulder bag and withdrew a grenade. "I've got just two of them. One for the fence—"

"Okay. But first tell me something. Why'd you come up here?"

"To help you rescue Emily," she replied. "Maybe to talk you out of doing something foolish, risking your life unnecessarily. Why? What difference does it make?"

She pulled the pin and lobbed the grenade. They flattened themselves on the ground as the grenade rolled to the fence and exploded. Electricity arced and crackled as the broken fence wire bounced and tangled. The lights in the house went out, and abruptly the arcing stopped.

Bolan ran forward and jumped through the gap in the fence, followed closely by Yvette. Bullets kicked up holes in the ground around them. Someone was firing from behind the guardhouse at the gate in the now-dead fence. Whoever the sniper was, he was too damned good. Bolan leveled the Beretta on the guardhouse and fired a sustained burst. The little wooden building flew apart, and the hardman behind it staggered a few feet and fell.

A group of Iranians charged across the grass. Yvette swept them with a burst, taking three of them down.

One man got to his feet and continued to fire. Bolan dropped him.

The burst of slugs from the Frenchwoman's Beretta had slammed into the Iranians' legs. The men were wounded, but alive. The man who had led the charge hauled himself to his knees and emptied his magazine into Yvette. Bolan took him and the other Iranian out of play with a spray of autofire that nearly tore the corpses in two. He then rolled close to Yvette, got to his knees and bent over her prostrate form. Blood ran from the woman's mouth. She was dead.

But the warrior had no time to mourn. He yanked open Yvette's nylon bag, grabbed the second grenade and hung it in his belt. He took the time to shove one of her spare magazines into his Beretta, then hauled out the two last magazines and dropped them in his sack.

A clump of grass to his left was kicked into the air by a stream of slugs. A Corsican hardman had thrown himself prone in the remains of the laboratory and was trying to pick Bolan off. The guy was shielded by the rubble, and it wouldn't be easy to get him. Bolan jumped up and ran toward the wreckage of the guardhouse, dropping behind the fallen pile of lumber.

The body of the hardman he'd chopped down lay a few feet away. The lumber didn't shield Bolan, any more than it had shielded the Corsican, but it hid him from sight. The hardman in the lab rubble spewed rounds into the ruins of the little wooden house, splintering boards, kicking up dust. Bolan slid forward on his belly to avoid being hit.

The hardman continued to pour autofire in Bolan's direction. But he'd have to stop to change magazines. When he stopped firing, Bolan stood and loosed a deadly stream of bullets, which caught the guy across the chest and lifted him off his feet. The high-velocity punch drove him backward and onto the ground in an untidy heap.

Until now most of the hardmen had ignored Bolan, leaving it to a picked squad to take care of the one- or two-man assault from the eastern fence. They were busy loading the cars and vans, preparing to charge down the lane and away. They had no desire to shift their attention to a perimeter skirmish. Now they saw that someone had penetrated the compound, had killed ten or twelve of their men and was a real threat. Someone yelled orders, and a new squad assembled. Bolan had their complete and undivided attention.

THE MAN IN CHARGE was Andres Kostenjevac. He was furious that Muro had left him behind, giving the girl the seat in the Storch that should have been his. It was Kostenjevac who had ordered the loading of heroin and morphine base into the Mercedes. If he survived this night, he meant to be a very wealthy man. Let the padrone lay claim to it! To hell with the padrone!

He hadn't dared to speak any such words to the grim, murderous Corsicans who had arrived at the compound today. They called themselves men of honor. If they had to die to save the organization, to save its leader, they would, though not gladly. It was a price they had always known they might have to pay for the good life they had lived for many years, and they were ready to pay it if they had to.

But maybe they wouldn't have to perish if they could break out of here. All of them knew scores of places where they could retreat, hide, wait. All they needed was a few minutes' head start on the pursuing police—and that they damned well meant to have.

It had been easy enough to encourage an Iranian to volunteer to drive the van that would blast open the roadblock. He was in the house now, on his rug, praying. The man was happy. He felt privileged.

The Iranian would drive the van to the first roadblock, showing a white flag on his radio antenna. When he was at the block, he would detonate the ample supply of plastique that had been loaded in the van. The two cars and the other vans would then plow through, taking advantage of the surprise and chaos that would surely result from the tremendous blast. Then, unless the police had set up their roadblocks in double depth, the roads would be clear for a dash out of the area.

Kostenjevac guessed that he needed about a two-minute lead. If he had that, he could drive the powerful blue Mercedes well ahead of all pursuers, while the Renault and the vans scattered, confusing the pursuit. He needed fifteen minutes to reach a safehouse where he could hide the car and himself. Before the night was over, he would be on his way in another car, in farmer's clothes, to another safehouse much farther away.

But he hadn't counted on so early an intrusion inside the perimeter fence by so effective a gunman. Mack Bolan wasn't a myth after all, it would appear. That was why he had given the orders for a dozen men, if it took that many, to lay down a field of fire no man could survive. They faced the shattered little gatehouse now, lining up with their submachine guns, firing sporadic bursts. In a moment they would fire together, on the command of Fonza, the man he had put in charge. No man, or phantom, would survive.

BOLAN SWEPT across the forming line of hardmen with a stream of slugs from the Beretta, and suddenly their plan was no good. Four men fell; two backed away. Three stood their ground and returned fire. He had to roll fast to escape the bullets that tore into the ground where he had been. He was on his back and threw the Beretta over his shoulder to fire. He missed them, but his gunfire unsettled them long enough for him to roll onto his belly and get off an effective burst. Another man fell.

The magazine was empty. The two survivors stalked toward him, muzzles leveled, scanning the wreckage of the guardhouse and the nearby shrubbery for a sign of the man they meant to blow away before he could re-load. But Bolan wasn't reloading. The first shot from his Luger drilled one Corsican through the head. The remaining hardman had seen the muzzle blast and turned his weapon toward Bolan. The second shot blasted through the bridge of the guy's nose, blowing his head apart.

Bolan scrambled across the unpaved lane, across the face of the gate and dived to the ground on the grass to the west of the lane. Bullets pinged around him, but his adversaries were at a distance now, in the house or garage or firing from behind the cars and vans. He pulled the second grenade off his belt.

The problem now was that if he set off the explosives in the van, he might not survive the blast himself. He crawled on elbows and knees into the narrow space between the fence and the garage.

Muro's forces knew where he was. They were moving down to the fence on the other side of the lane, from where they would have a clear field of fire into the space where Bolan lay on the ground. He had only seconds to move.

Bolan pulled the pin, rose to his feet, trotted to the corner of the garage and heaved the grenade toward the van loaded with plastique. He raced back, grabbed the Beretta, leaped the fence and threw himself into the woods. He crouched behind the trunk of the largest tree he could reach.

The big trunk suddenly snapped hard into Bolan's back, sprawling him onto the ground, while limbs and leaves rained on and around him and a wall of noise hammered his eardrums. The instant vacuum created by the explosion sucked the air from his lungs and bile from his stomach, making him gasp and choke. Debris whistled through the air above him—steel mostly, the bodies and engines of the vans and cars, but also the brick, stone and splintered wood of the garage. As his lungs filled again, they drew in more fumes than air, and he coughed painfully. Bolan tried to roll under the tangle of limbs and found that he was pinned. He struggled and managed to lift his head enough to look toward the compound.

The house had collapsed, devastated by the force of the blast. The garage, the cars and vans were simply gone. Engine parts lay scattered across the lawn; twisted steel dangled from tree limbs. The moonlit scene was eerily silent.

Bolan heaved and struggled in his prison of debris. He realized that a branch lying over his legs had prevented a falling chunk of steel from slicing across him like a blade. The branch was still attached to the splintered trunk and had formed an effective beam to protect him. He wasn't pinned down, just entangled in a jumble of fallen tree. He wrenched himself loose and managed to stand.

The French were finally arriving. Bolan could see the blue lights on their vehicles, flashing in the roadside trees down the lane. Still cautious, they were advancing in force.

Bolan crossed the lane and ran to where Yvette's body lay as the first of the police entered the compound. Twenty men in riot gear, with shields and helmets, heavy weapons at the ready, advanced in a skirmish line.

"Over here!" Bolan yelled.

Three policemen rushed over to the man who knelt over the fallen woman, and looked down menacingly, somehow detached from human reality behind the Plexiglas shields that covered their faces.

"Yvette Duclos," Bolan said quietly. "Police Judiciare. Where's Inspector Grimmaud?"

One of them used his hand radio, and in a moment a car with flashing blue lights swung into the compound. Grimmaud was out before the vehicle came to a stop. He made his way through the debris and among the bodies. He, too, knelt by Yvette.

"Why, Bolan?" he demanded. "Why?"

"To save your butt, Grimmaud," Bolan said. "The explosion was supposed to go off at one of your roadblocks." He glanced around. "The scattered bodies would have been the bodies of your policemen and soldiers. When Yvette realized what was going on she decided to help."

"Where is Muro?"

"Gone. He escaped in a small plane and took Emily Grant with him."

"With a hundred kilos of pure heroin, no doubt."

Bolan shook his head. "I doubt it. He had Emily and the pilot. I don't think the plane could have carried another hundred kilos. Anyway, there was a hell of a lot of it blown up."

Grimmaud rose to his feet. "Yvette... She was a good woman. A good police agent, a—"

"Yeah," Bolan agreed. "And so is Emily Grant. I have a score to settle with Muro."

"There is no point in my telling you how to go about it."

"None whatsoever," Bolan replied.

They walked toward the ruins of the house. The police had rounded up a few prisoners, some injured. Grimmaud stared at the bodies lying on the ground.

Every man lay beside an automatic weapon, some with Skorpion machine pistols, some with Uzis.

Bolan pointed to a group of prisoners. "Look who's survived. The woman who stared at Yvette and me over lunch at the Byblos."

"Giovanna Sestri," Grimmaud said. "We will take great pleasure in questioning that woman at headquarters."

They walked toward the police van and watched the big, grim policeman fastening the prisoners' hands behind their backs with heavy handcuffs. They kept the muttering Giovanna Sestri outside the van. She would be taken away in a car.

A uniformed police officer with white hair and a bristling white mustache approached Grimmaud. Bolan couldn't read French police insignia, but this man was obviously of high rank. "Is this the American?" he asked Grimmaud.

"Yes, sir. Mack Bolan. Bolan, this is Monsieur le Directeur Fouçade."

"I am honored to meet you, Mr. Bolan." Director Fouçade bowed slightly. "We know of your work."

"I know of yours," Bolan replied.

Fouçade frowned. "And where is Kostenjevac?" he asked Grimmaud.

"Is he not among the prisoners?"

"No. I want every body examined," Fouçade told him. "We must know if Kostenjevac survived."

Grimmaud spoke to Bolan. "I hadn't told you this, Bolan, but they killed Thuret. And his daughter. It was probably Kostenjevac who did it. An evil man. One of Muro's chief lieutenants, often his executioner.''

"The girl did nothing."

"Except that she saw who killed her father," Director Fouçade replied dryly. "Incidentally, Mr. Bolan, you were here when Yvette Duclos was killed. Was she, by any chance, killed by anyone who survived?"

Bolan fastened an angry eye on Giovanna Sestri, who stood with her hands cuffed behind her, snapping obscenities at the officers near her, spitting at them. "No. Yvette's killer is dead.

"I need your help, *monsieur*," Bolan continued. "I'm going to rescue Emily Grant."

"And kill Vittorio Muro, I should imagine."

"It might happen in the process."

"You'll have help." He reached for Bolan's hand and gripped it. "*Bonne chance,* Monsieur Bolan. Good luck."

16

"I know what you're going to do. I know you'll tell me to go to hell if I try to give you an order not to do it. I won't even try to give you an order, even though that's what I'm supposed to do. The man has powerful friends. I mean, we got a call from the White House."

Mack Bolan sat across a round table from Duncan Martin, who was Bob Millard's replacement. They were in Nice. Saint-Tropez, Martin had said, was too small a town for men who needed to preserve their anonymity. They were meeting in a safehouse in a suburb, behind closed curtains.

Martin had impressed Bolan as a bureaucrat—at first, until he observed his precautions and listened to him talk. Fox Den did seem to recruit good men.

"Anyway, Emily might be dead," Martin went on. "In fact, it's likely she is."

"I don't think so," Bolan replied. "If he left Kostenjevac and his sister-in-law behind and took Emily in the plane instead, obviously he wants to keep her alive. If he wanted her dead, he would have killed her and taken one of them with him. She's important to him. She's his hostage."

"Maybe he wanted to torture her, or drug her, to find out as much as he could about Fox Den," Martin suggested. "He has a reputation for—I mean, you know he won't hesitate to drug her if he thinks he can learn anything that way. The man plays rough."

"It wouldn't do him much good. You know how much she knew. Everything operated on a need-to-know basis. I'm the only one who—"

"That's one reason why we're a little nervous about your venturing alone onto the island of Corsica," Martin said. "A whole island, Bolan, a whole island loyal to the padrone. Corsican loyalty is fiercer than Sicilian. Have you ever run across it before?"

Bolan shrugged. "Give my regards to the President."

"Actually, as I was about to tell you, the word from the Man is that you should use your own judgment, but that you should know how powerful the man is and not run wild into something tougher than you expected. My orders to try to stop you came from somebody else. You can imagine who. The President didn't consult him. The President just sends word to be very, very careful. He wouldn't like to lose you."

"Thanks."

"And that's the word from Hal Brognola. Be very, very careful."

"And keep it very, very quiet," Bolan added. "Because Muro has politicians in his pocket in every country, and there'll be an outcry if they figure it out that someone in the employ of the U.S. government took out Vittorio Muro. Some of them will have to start living on their salaries."

"You know more than I do," Martin said curtly.

"There was a time when politicians were among the chief assets of the old Cosa Nostra. When that became a scandal, they couldn't buy them as readily. Even if they paid more. The Corsicans are a lot smarter, a lot more subtle than the Sicilians ever were. They have some pretty important people in their pockets, through one means and another—money, blackmail... Muro funded the White Front, and there were some pretty powerful and prominent people mixed up in that. I understand what the President needs."

"He ordered us to give you something," Martin said. "Come out to the garage. I'll show you."

In the garage beside the little house, Martin opened the trunk of a green Jaguar and lifted out a long, narrow wooden box. He and Bolan knelt on the floor and pried off the lid.

"Recognize it?" Martin asked.

Lying in the box, cradled in a plastic bed shaped to fit it, was a rifle. Bolan shook his head. He'd never seen a weapon quite like it before.

"It's brand-new," Martin told him. "Experimental so far. You had better take it in the house and examine it, take it apart, put it together, familiarize yourself with it. I'm afraid you won't have a chance to practice firing it, but it's been sighted in, and the Army sharpshooter who did it told me it's the most accurate rifle he ever held in his hands. It's even better than a Weatherby, and you know how good one of those is. It's called a Weiss, after the guy who developed it. The President authorized the release of this one to you."

In the house Bolan examined the new rifle, which he saw was a masterpiece of design. It would fire special, hand-loaded ammunition, the powder having been meticulously weighed for each cartridge, so each bullet would fly precisely the same trajectory. Some of the bullets had explosive heads, the kind specifically outlawed by international law, and therefore used by no one but terrorists. The rifle was equipped with a folding steel stock, and the sound suppressor and flash concealer could be unscrewed and carried in clips on the stock, so the whole weapon was compact for carrying. It had two scopes, readily interchangeable: one a fine telescopic sight for daylight long-distance shooting, the other a sniper scope that enabled a man to aim in the dark. Everything fit into a shaped steel case that could be slung over a shoulder and carried without hampering a man's movements. The whole thing, rifle, ammo, scopes and case, weighed less than four kilograms.

"I've got something else for you. A present from Hal Brognola."

Another wooden box. Bolan pried off the lid and lifted out a .44 Desert Eagle. He hefted the weapon, thankful to have the familiar weight and feel of the flesh-shredder in his possession once again. There were fifty rounds of the special hand-loaded ammunition the big automatic required, as well as a quick-draw holster. Hal was a thoughtful, resourceful man.

"Hal said you favor .44s."

"I sure as hell do," Bolan replied. "But I'm going to keep the Lahti, too—the Finnish pistol the French gave me. I'm developing a real respect for that gun."

"Is there anything else I can do for you? Officially or unofficially?"

"Keep everybody out of the way," Bolan growled. "I don't want a police assault on Muro's villa about the time I'm working my way in."

BOLAN SNATCHED a few hours' sleep that afternoon, ate and spent the evening hours being briefed by French police agents. They showed him maps and aerial photographs. Some of the pictures of Muro's mountain villa had been taken that day, from high-flying planes. The French police were furious over the death of Yvette Duclos, and they savored the idea of Bolan slipping into the villa and killing Muro—something they wouldn't have to explain to the Président de la République or anyone else. The French weren't shy about police tactics, and they wouldn't be shy about denying they'd even so much as heard of him, if he failed, but they plainly envied Bolan his independence.

"We understand you are accustomed to working unofficially," Director Fouçade said.

"That's the way I work."

"Of course. And you will not be surprised, if it should be necessary, to hear us protest we have never heard of you."

"Worse than that," Bolan replied. "Your government may protest that a renegade American agent has murdered a respected citizen of Corsica."

The Frenchman nodded. "It is quite possible that is what will happen."

A PILOT HIRED by Police Judiciare agreed to drop Bolan in the Corsican mountains just before dawn. But sunrise was a long time away and Bolan had time to kill. Bolan returned to Byblos Hotel, took a long, hot shower and went down to the dining room for a quick meal. He pushed his food around his plate and barely tasted the small amount of fish that he ate. He didn't feel like eating, even though he knew he needed sustenance. His mind was on Corsica.

At a nearby table a man in his sixties fondled a girl of twenty as they did exactly what he couldn't—savor good food and drink, enjoy the candlelight, the summer evening. Bolan took notice of the contrast. At another table one of the photographers and two of the models who had known Yvette fell silent when they caught sight of Bolan. He looked at them, but they refused to meet his gaze. They didn't know what they resented, but they resented something and guessed it was him. They had no one else on whom to fix their anger, so the American made a good target. An old story.

Bolan was too edgy and uncomfortable to linger over his meal. He decided to take a short drive, maybe out to Tahiti Beach and back, thinking it might relieve his tension a little.

The BMW was back, parked in the hotel garage. He checked all around it before he unlocked and opened the door. He raised the hood and checked underneath before he switched on the ignition. The car was clean. He drove out of the garage and down the hill into the town, then out onto the road leading out the little peninsula and to the beach.

Plage de Tahiti wasn't deserted at night. A crowd, mostly of young people, ate and drank on the sand; many of them were quite drunk, many of them quite nude.

Bolan toyed with the idea of stripping off and going for a swim, except that he was carrying the Lahti in a harness under his jacket; and, oddly, he was seized by an oppressive instinct that it wouldn't be a good idea to leave the gun in the car and go walking on the beach without it. Fully dressed, he walked across the wide parking lot to the edge of the sand, and stood looking out at the water, where a few boats rocked in a gentle swell, and at the cavorting, laughing couples on the sand.

He turned away and walked back through the parking lot to the BMW, between cars where couples were— *coupling* was the way to put it. He got in behind the wheel. Cold steel prodded his neck.

"Don't turn around, Bolan."

In the five minutes he had been gone, someone had opened the locked car and hidden in the rear seat. Now that same someone held a pistol to his neck—someone with an odd accent that Bolan couldn't identify. He drew a deep breath, then let it out.

"Okay, pal. You call the shots."

"You're damn right I do. So drive, Bolan. Slow. Don't make any quick moves. We're leaving here."

Bolan started the car and drove carefully out of the parking lot, onto the narrow, traffic-crowded road that led back to Saint-Tropez.

"Don't you want to know who I am?" asked the man in the rear seat.

"Let me guess. You're Andres Kostenjevac, right?"

"Very good."

"How did you escape last night?" Bolan asked. "I mean, after the padrone abandoned you—"

"And you ruined my alternative plan. Well... A man of your experience, Bolan, would know that a man who wants to survive—and, believe me, I *have* survived a hell of a lot—always prepares more than one way out. When you blew up the van of explosives, I didn't wait to see what was going to happen to whom. I went."

"Through the line the French police and army had thrown around the compound?"

"If I allowed you to turn around, you would see I am in the uniform of a policeman. I had it hidden in a car."

"So why have you taken the trouble of—"

"Oh, it's very simple, Bolan," Kostenjevac said coldly. "I have a reputation to maintain. It is known that people who cross me wind up—"

"Dead," Bolan finished the sentence.

"Dead," Kostenjevac confirmed. "Or without their balls. Occasionally without their kneecaps."

"How about Vittorio Muro? He crossed you, didn't he? Strange how he valued the girl more than you."

"Not strange," Kostenjevac replied. "She's the bait in the trap he's setting for you."

"But you won't let me fall into that trap, will you?"

"No. You're going to be my safe conduct into the padrone's villa. I will come bearing evidence. '*Signor*, I've finished off the Executioner.' What do I carry to him, Bolan? A Polaroid picture of your corpse? I tell you what is strange, Bolan. Until last night I believed you were a myth. Anyway, the padrone will be grateful. He'll let down his guard. And then... Then I will demonstrate that even Vittorio Muro can't cross Andres Kostenjevac."

They were approaching an intersection.

"Turn right."

"Up into the hills?"

"Up into the hills," Kostenjevac repeated.

Traffic was lighter on the road north. Kostenjevac relaxed a notch and no longer held the muzzle of his pistol to Bolan's neck. Bolan glanced in the rearview mirror, and in the light from the headlights of an approaching car he could see the man's face. Sure. Distinctive. He'd seen him before. Kostenjevac was the man who had sat with Giovanna Sestri for a poolside lunch at the Byblos.

That day Bolan had focused on the woman and hadn't paid attention to the man, but it was him, no question. Another headlight shone through the windshield, and Bolan took a second look at Kostenjevac. He saw a man who was tense and alert but not nervous, unafraid. Kostenjevac was a man who could kill quite calmly.

Yeah. Maybe even with the pleasure a few men take in killing. And he would do it as soon as they reached a less-traveled part of the road, a place where he could shoot Bolan, push the body out and drive away.

Soon. There wasn't much time, and not much room to maneuver. Kostenjevac was a cool hit man. He would be quick, ruthless and deadly. He anticipated some such simple dodge as a jab at the brakes, a twist of the wheel. He was braced for that. Whatever Bolan did, it had to be something better.

One thing... Kostenjevac wasn't wearing a seat belt. In fact, there weren't any in the rear seat of this European BMW. It was equipped with seat belts with shoulder harnesses in front, and out of habit Bolan had fastened his. An advantage. Maybe the only one he had.

Bolan pressed down on the accelerator, and the BMW picked up speed.

"No deal we could make?" the warrior asked. "I'd just as soon live, if we could come to some kind of arrangement."

"What kind of arrangement could it be?" the man asked.

"Well, I thought—" Bolan began just as he whipped the wheel to the right.

Accelerating through forty mph, the BMW slammed into a steel-reinforced concrete utility pole. The sudden turn had already snapped Bolan's shoulder harness tight. Though he moved hardly at all, his breath exploded from him as his chest pulled against the hard restraint of the nylon belt. Kostenjevac was hurled over the back of the front seat and into the dashboard and windshield.

Bolan was stunned, but not so stunned that he didn't hear Kostenjevac shrieking curses and fumbling for his pistol. The man was injured, and mad with pain and fury. Bolan looked for the pistol, but couldn't see it. He fumbled with the buckle on the seat belt and released himself from the harness. Then he forced the bent door open and rolled out of the BMW, onto the ground beside the roadway.

The lights of an approaching car swept over the wrecked vehicle. Lying on his back, gasping for air, Bolan looked up at the battered hit man. In the white glare of the headlights his blood-streaked face was the apparition of a devil. One eye was torn and bloody and already beginning to puff shut; his nose was smashed flat; blood ran from his mouth; a gurgling roar issued from that ruined mouth, spewing blood and flesh.

But Kostenjevac had found his pistol and now raised it in two trembling hands. He lowered the muzzle toward Bolan and got off a shot. When the slug tore into the ground not a foot from Bolan's belly, Kostenjevac slowly moved the muzzle to take better aim.

A 9 mm slug from the Lahti tore up through Kostenjevac's throat and shattered the base of his skull. Fragments of brain splattered on the ceiling of the BMW.

AFTER MIDNIGHT Bolan checked his equipment again—knives, a canteen of water, a coil of nylon rope, two cylinders that would launch signal rockets five or six hundred feet in the air, his two pistols, the Weiss rifle and ammunition. A little after 2:00 a.m. he climbed into a single-engine, high-wing airplane. He'd make the parachute jump into Corsica just before dawn.

He was lucky in one respect. The weather had turned sullen. A low cloud formation hung over the Mediterranean, so there was no moonlight. The little plane flew low over the water. It was the kind of flying pilots called scud-running, and it was dangerous, but this pilot knew what he was doing. As he sat beside the pilot in the noisy cockpit, Bolan checked his parachute harness and wondered if the clouds were so low they would hide the mountain slope he had chosen for his landing.

The plane was slow and required more than an hour to reach the island. They crossed the coastline just west of the village of Saint-Florent. Mountains loomed ahead of them. As the land rose, the clouds seemed to hang lower, and it was as if they were flying into an immense mouth. Both men scanned the dark landscape below, looking for the landmarks they had identified on the maps and photographs before take off. They had to shout to hear each other over the roar of the engine.

There were few landmarks. The villages below showed only a light here and there; roads looked alike. The pilot was flying a compass course, based on the last landmark he recognized, while Bolan searched for others. The distance between clouds and land diminished every minute.

They wouldn't fly over Muro's villa, even if they could. A low-flying small plane, in the half-light before dawn, would only serve to alert the guards. The landing site was a mountain meadow about three miles from the villa, far enough away that the pass by the plane wouldn't be noticed. Bolan had chosen this particular meadow because of a distinctive pattern of nearby groves that would identify it unmistakably. In the photographs, the meadow looked suitably isolated, so in the absence of a piece of bad luck, he'd make his landing unnoticed.

Their timing was right. Although the sun wasn't due to rise for another three-quarters of an hour, the sky was beginning to turn to pale gray in the east. It afforded them enough light to see the landscape below, vague and misty but sufficiently defined to be identified.

"There!" Bolan shouted into the ear of the pilot. He had spotted the pattern of trees. "Just to the left. You see?"

The pilot nodded and turned into a slow, tilting pass over the meadow.

They were flying in the very edge of the overhanging clouds, indeed sometimes passing through shreds of wet mist and for a moment losing sight of the ground. The pilot guided the plane down a final fifty feet. Bolan unbuckled his seat belt and opened the door, swung his legs out and took a grip on the door frame. He planted a foot on the bottom of the door frame and another on the wing strut.

He watched the ground below him, not more than a thousand feet away. The mountainside, wet with morning fog, was a landscape in tones of gray. Nothing was distinct. He judged the best he could as the plane passed over a grove of trees. That was it, the odd-shaped grove—the landmark. The pilot gestured and grinned. Bolan nodded curtly.

The pilot reached out and put a hand on Bolan's arm, then gave a thumbs-up sign. *"Bonne chance!"* he yelled as Bolan flung himself into the void.

There was no time to play games with the parachute. He pulled the rip cord immediately, and the black chute blossomed out, forming a big round canopy above his head. It slowed his fall just in time. Jumping from this altitude, he had only seconds before his feet plowed into the wet meadow grass and the mud beneath. He was on the ground before the plane disappeared into the clouds to the north, its small engine barely audible on the ground.

No lights flashed on; no one shouted. The warrior stood, peering around, alert. Nothing. It looked as if he'd managed to land on Corsica with no one the wiser.

So far, so good. There was no wind to impede his effort to collapse the parachute. He gathered it up and carried it away, heading for the cover of the nearest trees.

The airplane came around, gliding with its engine throttled back almost to total silence. It was a stupid move, as far as Bolan was concerned, but the pilot probably wanted to assure himself his parachutist hadn't broken a leg on landing. Bolan waved as the plane passed overhead, and the pilot rocked his wings. Then he eased in the throttle, and the engine made a little noise. He had to do that to climb. Bolan crouched on the ground, waiting for a sign that indicated someone had heard. Again, nothing. He was alone.

In the grove he crammed the parachute into the smallest bundle possible and hid it in the bush. He took a minute to check his equipment. Nothing had been damaged.

Bolan took out a compass and checked directions. If he had landed in the meadow identified on the aerial photos, the villa was about three miles from here, 170 degrees. The more distance he covered before dawn, the less likely he would be discovered too soon, so he set off at a fast pace.

He wore camouflaged army fatigues and paratrooper boots. The cool morning was the best time for such hiking. He had figured he could cover three miles in an hour or a little more. But on the ground he found the terrain slightly more rugged than he had supposed, and he revised his estimate to an hour and a half.

He began his upward climb. The sun rose, at first glorious red, then white through the gradually dissipating mist, until it was high above the clouds, and the day was shadowless light. He checked his compass often and estimated his distance from the time. It felt good, climbing in the cool mountain air, and Bolan knew he was alert and strong. He would have enjoyed the hike under different circumstances.

And there it was, the villa, a formidable cluster of stone buildings near the mountaintop. When Bolan first caught sight of it from the crest of a little ridge he'd just topped, he stopped, impressed with the villa's grim and ancient beauty.

It was a fortress, though, and damned near impregnable. The padrone had chosen his site well. With a few men he could defend his mountaintop against a regiment.

Bolan knew he was exposed. He dropped to his belly, and, fixing the scope on the Weiss rifle, used it as a telescope.

There were shepherds among the sheep on the slope below the villa. Shepherds who carried submachine guns. Other armed hardmen paced the periphery of the villa. No Iranians here. The padrone was guarded by his own kind.

The warrior scanned the mountain meadow and the herd of sheep through the scope of the Weiss. Two of the men were unarmed, real shepherds, he supposed. One of the hardmen appeared to be the leader. He moved from man to man, apparently giving orders. He was a thin, cruel-faced man, dressed in a black leather jacket open over a white shirt, tight straight-legged jeans and thin-soled Italian-style shoes—no shepherd, no mountain man, obviously. He smoked a thin cigar as he strode across the meadow, stopping for a moment at each man. He carried what looked to be an Uzi—certainly some type of machine pistol. And in a holster hanging from the belt of his jeans was an automatic pistol.

Bolan knew he could drop the guy easily. But first he wanted to find out one thing: who was that anonymous, distant man he was thinking about killing?

For sure the man was no innocent mountain shepherd. His weapons were evidence enough of that. The leader of a company of shepherds might carry a rifle to protect the sheep from wolves, but he didn't carry a machine pistol. No, this man was one of Muro's heaviest heavies, a gunman assigned to the defense of the villa, and if he hadn't killed anyone with those guns he carried, for damn sure he had killed many people by his faithful service to the padrone.

Yvette. Millard. Brigitte Thuret. That gunman shared in the responsibility for all of them—and for every man, woman and child who died as the result of the newly expanding commerce in deadly heroin.

The Weiss was a single-shot, bolt-action rifle. Bolan extracted a long, slender cartridge from his bag and inserted it into the breech. He shoved the bolt forward and turned down the knob. The Weiss was loaded.

He took aim on the Uzi-toting hardman. It was easy to estimate the distance. The scope mounted on the Weiss had a range finder, and he could adjust for the range by twisting a knob on its side. The adjustment was reflected in the movement of a needle in the field of the scope. As for windage, he had to estimate that, but the muzzle velocity of these slugs would be so great that anything short of a gale blowing across the mountainside should have little effect.

He decided not to kill him. Let the others see him drop and not know why. Putting a little fear in these Corsican thugs would be a good thing.

Bolan steadied the cross hairs on the hardman at hip level. He was a good three hundred yards away, so the front of the scope was dipped slightly toward the muzzle, and the muzzle was raised accordingly. Bolan watched the man shift from one foot to another, then stop and stand still.

He fired.

Bolan watched everything through the scope. The man shuddered, then staggered back a couple of steps, screaming. He threw his Uzi aside and fell on his back. As he rolled on the ground and screamed, his companions ran toward him. Two of them had the presence of mind to level their weapons and look around for the gunman who had fired on their leader. But they saw nothing. Bolan was farther away than they could have guessed, and they hadn't heard the faint grunt of his silenced rifle.

The hardmen ran for cover, leaving their leader rolling and screaming on the ground.

Bolan disassembled the Weiss and packed it in its case. He retreated behind the rim of the ridge and set out toward the north, to circle the villa from the direction away from the mountain road.

17

It was like stabbing a hornet's nest with a stick. Men poured out of the villa, angry and threatening, twenty or more of them, all heavily armed. Now they moved cautiously along the walls, dropping to the ground when they had to cover open ground, every man alert and ready. They moved with the stolid determination of trained troops—but with a difference. These men had been trained as killers, not soldiers. Their discipline was questionable.

The biggest problem for Muro's troops was that they didn't know where their attacker was. They didn't even know what direction the shots had come from, and they didn't know where to look.

Bolan had moved two hundred yards, just to be sure. He had another view of the villa, from the edge of a stand of evergreen brush two hundred yards to the north but as high on the mountainside as the villa itself. Through the scope he scanned the layout of buildings. It was apparent that the white, more modern house was where Muro lived. It was unlikely he lived in the ancient chapel or in one of the stone towers, or for that matter in the low-lying stone outbuildings that had in the past sheltered cattle and pigs and now served as garages, maybe as stores for ammunition.

One thing Bolan hadn't counted on. Looking down the mountain toward the village far below the villa, he could see a stirring. He should have remembered that Muro was the padrone here and, like any feudal lord, could call on his peasants for help. Probably he had, by radio or simply by telephone. The villagers were assembling in the streets, and it was likely they would start up the mountain on trucks. Within an hour, the mountainside might be swarming with a hundred of them. Bolan had thought in terms of a protracted siege. Now he guessed he had but little time.

From his new vantage point Bolan could see an armed man patrolling the courtyard in front of the main house, speaking into a hand-held radio. Bolan assembled the Weiss, loaded it and shot the man in the shoulder.

He could hear the Corsican hardmen yelling. They began a general retreat into the courtyard, into the building, moving fast, just short of panic. He picked off two more, just to reduce the odds before they established their standoff. They would go for cover and wouldn't dare come out. But he would be outside, unable to touch them except by moving in. And that was *his* big problem.

He circled back the way he had come, to the east of the villa. As alert as they now were, no one had yet spotted him. He remained a complete mystery to them. They knew what they were up against, no doubt—a man named Mack Bolan, called the Executioner. He had wounded two of them, including an important leader, and wounded or killed two more, and they didn't even know from what direction he was firing.

Bolan heard someone start up an engine. He loaded one of the explosive-tipped bullets into the Weiss, adjusted the sight for the distance between him and the road and waited. Sure enough, a big black car roared through the gap in the ruined wall, skidded onto the road and sped down the mountain. Bolan aimed at the gas tank, hit it with the exploding bullet and watched the car erupt in flame. Two people leaped out of the burning vehicle. It wasn't Muro with Emily. Maybe it had been a test to see if they could get away.

The driver and his companion crawled away from the car, bellying back toward the villa. Bolan let them go. He had no reason to think they were killers.

Standoff again. Bolan trotted north, keeping low behind the ridge and out of sight from the villa. He climbed into the low evergreen brush on the slope above. That was where he had his best view—he could see through some of the windows. He put a healthy fear into two or three armed men and a woman inside one room by popping an explosive bullet through their window, to explode against a wall inside.

As soon as the round left his rifle, Bolan moved. If they were smart enough to figure angles—

A bullet kicked up dirt two feet from where he crouched. He spun around and needed a moment to locate the gunman. A Corsican thug was taking aim at him with a big revolver, from about sixty yards away. He got off another shot before Bolan could react, but he missed. Few men could fire accurately with a pistol at sixty or seventy yards—even accurately enough to hit a man. Someone who had killed with a pistol at ten feet might think he could hit at any distance, but it wasn't so; he couldn't. Bolan could, because he was a marksman who had practiced long to achieve accuracy with his weapons. He aimed the Lahti and dropped the Corsican with his first shot.

A small vehicle roared up the mountain, a Fiat loaded with many more men than it was meant to carry. Perimeter guards, summoned back to the defense of the fort? If he could have been sure of that, he'd have fired through the windshield. But they could have been villagers, hurrying to see what was wrong at the villa. When they scrambled out of the Fiat it was clear that these were more of Muro's troops. The warrior took out two of them as they ran toward the shelter of the ruined chapel.

The President's gift of the Weiss rifle was proving more valuable than he could have guessed.

How was he going to move in? Emily was inside, and if he didn't take the initiative, he couldn't hope to do anything for her. But between the nearest cover and the walls of the villa was a hundred yards of flat, open land, which would give twenty men with automatic weapons a clear shot at him when he began his run. He had no hope of making it.

He—

"Bolan! It is Bolan, isn't it? I have your girl friend. Do you want her?" Accented English blared through a bullhorn. "Bolan! Show yourself. We won't fire on you. We can come to an accommodation. Your girl is well. Unharmed. The three of us can leave here together. We will separate when we have reached safety. It is a reasonable proposition. I understand you are a reasonable man."

It was the final bluff by a frightened man, and the way to handle it was simply to keep silent. Not to answer with a shot. Not to offer any evidence that he had heard at all.

Of course they would try him. In time they would put him to some kind of test.

"Bolan! I have reinforcements coming. Do you? I have the trump card. Do you want this young woman alive? Bolan? Do you want her alive?"

He kept silent. It was a war of nerves.

"Bolan?"

Two hardmen ventured out through the gap in the old wall, weapons ready, nervously alert. Volunteers. It seemed a shame to kill two men so foolishly brave. He slipped an exploding bullet into the chamber of the Weiss and fired it into the ground between them. They scrambled back to safety.

"All right, Bolan. I have your message. Do you want to see her? You don't believe I have her? Don't believe she's alive and well? All right. I'll show you."

There was a broad terrace on the northeast front of the house. Access from the house was by way of a pair of tall glass doors. Those doors opened.

Emily came out first, held from behind by Muro. She wasn't handcuffed, as Bolan had last seen her, but she was still wearing the white bikini, and her ankles were shackled together with a pair of leg irons. Muro's left arm was around her waist. In his right hand he held a heavy nickel-plated revolver, likely a .357 Magnum.

Muro wrestled Emily out to the middle of the terrace, and he stood there, holding her before him as a shield, brandishing the pistol. He yelled something, but without the bullhorn his voice couldn't carry to Bolan, who was still about two hundred yards away.

Another standoff. Muro was wrestling Emily around, maybe because she was struggling against him, maybe because he wanted Bolan to see her punished. Even through the scope Bolan couldn't tell which.

It seemed like a good time to send a message, though. Bolan took very careful aim and fired a shot that exploded a wineglass on a table two feet from Muro's belly.

Muro began to push Emily back toward the door, but suddenly he rose awkwardly off the ground, like a limp rag doll lifted by a child. Emily had bent down and risen up under him, hoisting him on her shoulders, and in an instant she slammed him hard on his back on the tile.

Surprised and hurt, he struggled to rise, but she chopped him on the throat with her right hand, and with her left she twisted the revolver out of his grip.

She scrambled backward, into the corner between the white stucco wall of the house and the low north wall of the terrace, where she was protected from fire from almost any direction.

Muro lay still on his back. A man burst through the glass doors, and Emily shot him in the chest. He grabbed at the wound and stumbled backward, falling against the padrone and bloodying his suit. Another man jumped onto the terrace, only to be caught by Bolan's next shot from the superaccurate rifle. The hardman staggered back inside, then fell forward and sprawled on the floor of the terrace.

And there it stood. Muro lay on his back, conscious, gasping. Two Corsicans lay bleeding on the tiles. Emily crouched in the shelter of two walls.

The nature of the standoff had changed radically. Now, in some sense, Bolan and Emily had a hostage— Muro. But they were outgunned, and she was in an extremely dangerous position, backed into a corner where no one could fire on her, but unable to leave.

Bolan laid out explosive ammunition on the ground beside him. The Corsicans, once again like angry hornets, ran from door to door, from building to building, appearing in one window after another, looking for a place where they could get off a shot at Emily. Bolan picked off another one. Emily had to conserve her ammunition.

A Corsican leaned out a window above the terrace. Bolan shot him. Someone fired a shot from the same window. The bullet shattered a tile on the terrace but ricocheted harmlessly away from Emily. The windows were at the wrong angle for shooting at her, unless a man leaned out far enough.

Bolan scanned the windows, watching for someone else to make a move. One did. Bolan's explosive bullet hit him in the head, spraying blood over the white stucco around the window.

Emily couldn't move. Bolan, too, had to stay put, for fear of leaving her unprotected for even a moment.

Muro lay on his back within arm's reach of Emily. She saw the advantage in that and reached forward and hauled him to her, jerking him by one foot. Through the scope Bolan could see Muro protest. Emily pressed the muzzle of the big revolver to his temple. Muro lay back, quiet.

Bolan held another card in his hand. He removed one of the signal flares from his pack. Holding it to fire straight up, he jammed down the detonator. The little rocket flew out of the tube and up five hundred feet, where it burst with a flash and then hung on a parachute and began to drift down, burning with a fierce red flame and emitting thick white smoke. It was a light signal at night, a smoke signal by day, and the French police were supposed to be watching for it. When it burned out, he fired the second one.

The bullhorn clattered across the floor of the terrace, thrown out to Emily and Muro. Muro grabbed it.

"Bolan! It hasn't changed. She is still my hostage. If she harms me, they will rush her and kill her painfully. We can make a deal."

Emily grabbed the bullhorn from his hands. Bolan couldn't understand everything she said—she spoke rapidly in Italian—but he gathered from the words he could understand that she was threatening the Corsicans with the death of their padrone.

"Mack! Let 'em go to hell! We've got 'em by the short hairs."

The trucks were coming up the mountain. Reinforcements. Maybe fifty more Corsicans, well armed and angry. Bolan hadn't brought a submachine gun. If the Corsicans were bold enough to charge him en masse, he wouldn't be able to take down enough to stop them. They'd get him. And they were supposed to be lunatic enough to chance a charge.

He wished he could call down some words of encouragement to Emily, though he didn't know what they would be. Another hardman leaned out a window, and Bolan shot him in the shoulder.

The trucks rounded the last curve, and men began to jump off. Some of them were armed with submachine guns; others carried sawed-off shotguns. Every man had at least a pistol. They began to form squads.

Bolan's attention was drawn by the whup-whup of two helicopters, chopping along a hundred feet above the mountain slope, keeping under the clouds. The pilots *had* been watching, had seen his signal rockets. The helicopters skimmed the meadow to the east and opened fire on the four trucks with heavy machine guns.

At first it was obvious they only meant to drive the Corsicans back, not hit them.

But the Corsicans wouldn't retreat and knelt to return fire with everything they had. The choppers backed off, then swung their double machine guns toward the Corsicans and fired streams of tracers. At least a dozen men fell. Survivors ran behind the trucks and fired from there. One chopper circled at a distance and fired from the other side. The Corsican reinforcements broke and raced for the safety of the woods.

They were brave. Bolan had to admire them—simple, ignorant men, fighting and ready to die for their padrone without knowing why. It was a shame, but all he could think of right now was that their ignorant courage was dangerous. They meant to kill him and Emily.

Two more helicopters roared up the mountain, bigger ones with double rotors, carrying assault troops. They landed downslope from Bolan and began to form a line to move against the villa. These troops wore steel helmets and flak jackets, and they carried long automatic rifles.

Taking a chance that the hardmen in the villa would be staring at the helicopters and the forming assault, Bolan dropped the Weiss and ran down the slope toward the wall of the villa. He was correct about where their attention was focused, but even so, some spotted him and fired. Too late. Their slugs simply tore into the ground around him.

While their distraction lasted, Bolan jumped atop the old stone wall and dropped inside. Now, with the Desert Eagle in hand, he rushed against the back wall of an outbuilding and began to slip along toward the front of the house.

He heard a shot from the terrace. If the Corsicans realized he was no longer on the slope above, knocking off every man who showed a face at a window, Emily would have to protect herself until he reached her. And she couldn't have more than four shots left in the revolver. He shoved the .44 back into his holster. The sound-suppressed Lahti was what he needed now.

Two Corsicans had an idea where he was. One came around the old stable, now a garage, Uzi leveled. Bolan fired and the man dropped. The other one had come around the other way, which took him longer. Bolan anticipated him and was ready when the guy stepped out to fire. The impact of the 9 mm slug drove the gunner to the ground.

Bolan sprinted to the northeast corner of the house, just below the terrace. Heavy return fire was pouring from the windows, at the French assault force that was now beginning to move up the mountain slope.

"Emily!"

"Mack?"

"Can you jump over the edge and drop down here?"

"I suppose so."

"Well, do it. All hell's breaking loose."

Emily fired a single shot, then vaulted over and fell awkwardly to her knees on the ground beside him, her ankles still chained together.

She waved the nickel-plated revolver around in the air, frustrated that it was almost empty. Bolan handed her the Lahti and drew the Desert Eagle.

He led her along the foundation wall, away from where the Corsicans believed them to be. She could barely stumble along, her legs shackled with a short chain.

"You got another clip for this?" she asked, raising the Lahti. "And what the hell's that?" She jerked her head at the .44.

He handed her an extra 9 mm clip.

A burst of automatic fire kicked up the earth just beyond them. They still had some protection from the wall of the house, but that wasn't going to last long. Desperation and the wild courage born of desperation was goading the Corsicans.

Suddenly two hardmen jumped around the corner of the terrace, their Uzis chattering before they even knew where to aim. Bolan triggered a round from the Desert Eagle. The heavy slug punched a hole through the man and slammed him back. Emily's 9 mm stinger drilled into the other man's belly. He dropped his Uzi, and as he slumped to his knees she shot him through his mouth.

Another hardman stepped into plain sight. A shot from the Desert Eagle exploded the man's chest and drove him backward to where others beyond the wall could see him. Bolan knew how effective it was in a fight like this for thugs to see what a bloody mess a .44 slug made of a man. What was more, the roar of the big automatic echoed like thunder off the walls of the villa and off the mountainside.

"Behind!" Emily shrieked as she fired her weapon.

Bolan threw himself to the ground and rolled, coming up in a combat crouch with the .44 aimed and firing. One slug literally tore the arm off a hardman and went on to cut down another one. Emily put a 9 mm round in the chest of the man whose arm hung on torn ligaments, and he fell to his knees, then slowly slumped to the ground.

And then it was quiet. At least it was comparatively quiet. Bolan and Emily stood as tense as coiled springs, listening, starting at every tiny sound, looking for the next hardman who would throw himself around a corner and open fire.

But it was over.

The French soldiers swarmed into the villa, unopposed. They began to round up the Corsicans.

An officer in khaki strode around the corner of the terrace. His men were dressed like paratroopers. He was dressed like a parade soldier. The man began to speak in the crisp tones adopted by the career soldiers of every army, and in English with hardly a trace of accent.

"Monsieur Bolan? Mademoiselle Grant? I am Major Leclerc. Let me be the first to congratulate you on your courage and the complete success of our combined operation. I have a helicopter ready to take you out of here immediately. You understand we must not allow anyone to know you were here, or why. It is all unofficial. Indeed—though I regret it—I will be compelled to say I have never heard of you, much less ever saw you. For this moment, I admire you beyond measure. Ten minutes from now..."

Bolan sheltered Emily in his arms. "Two things, Major," he said. "Something to cut the chains off the young lady. And—" he pointed up the slope "—I have a fine rifle up there that I don't want to leave behind."

Major Leclerc nodded. "A question. We have orders to take Vittorio Muro alive. Where is the padrone, can you tell me?"

Emily raised her chin. "I shot the son of a bitch."

EPILOGUE

A month later Mack Bolan and Emily Grant were the guests at a private dinner in Paris. Their host was Maurice Beaufort, Director-General of Sûreté Nationale. Present also were Inspector Grimmaud, Director Fouçade and Duncan Martin. The dinner was private, in an elegant dining room at the Ministry of the Interior. The wine, the food and the brandy were the best that France had to offer.

The French spoke of Yvette Duclos and Robert Millard and saluted them with solemn toasts. Then, after dinner, Director-General Beaufort spoke to them about the aftermath of the attack on the Corsican villa.

"You understand the story we released to the public?" he asked. "I mean, do you understand the motive? It worked, the story. It has achieved its purpose."

The news story released by the French government said that Shiite Muslims were infuriated at Vittorio Muro for using the forces of the Union Corse to frustrate their efforts to intrude into the European heroin trade. They had, it said, landed on the Corsican mountainside in Libyan helicopters and attacked the men in the villa.

This news story had been circulated throughout the world. Colonel Khaddafi protested vehemently, but nearly the whole world believed the story.

"As we had expected," Director-General Beaufort said with a little smile, "this story has inspired some of the ayatollahs to declare an Islamic Jihad against the Union Corse. A few fanatics have come, trying to win passage to heaven by murdering Corsicans."

"I suspect that has been a big mistake," Bolan observed.

"Every one has found his quick passage to heaven," Director Fouçade said. "And among the Corsicans... not a single casualty."

"Besides this," Beaufort continued, "the new hostility between the Union Corse and the Iranian Shiites has created some large difficulties for Muslim terrorists in Europe. They have become accident-prone, as we might say."

"But the heroin traffic," Emily said. "Did—"

"Better than we could have dreamed," Beaufort replied. "The stream has dried up. The traffic has had to return to the old sources. Heroin has become scarce and more costly.

"Also, you might be interested to know that Giovanna Sestri has taken up permanent residence in a prison in the northeast of France. She complains of the weather there, saying it is too cold for a civilized person."

"Someday she'll look back very fondly on the cool days and nights she spent there," Emily said. "It's supposed to be uncomfortably warm in hell."

Director-General Beaufort laughed heartily.

"But we have a problem," Martin told them. "Some members of the National Assembly here in France, and some members of Congress in the States, aren't satisfied with our explanation of Vittorio Muro's death. They're talking about a congressional investigation."

"We know how to lie," Emily replied bluntly. "We've been taught by experts and have developed a certain skill at it."

"It goes this far," Martin said. "A New Jersey congressman has so far gotten eighteen cosponsors on a House resolution to honor the memory of Vittorio Muro. They want ironclad assurance that no one in the United States government knows anything about how he died."

"Have you given it to them?" Emily asked.

Martin smiled, but it seemed painful for him to do so. "We have tried to avoid too definite a statement."

"Then...?"

"We think it would be well if you two were out of sight for a while. The government of France would like it, too, if you simply weren't available to answer questions. Have you ever thought of a nice vacation, say on a sunny beach, with nothing to worry about?"

"As guests of the government of France," Director-General Beaufort added. "On Tahiti. Or one of the nearby islands where it is even more unspoiled and peaceful."

"I have bruises that haven't yet healed," Emily murmured.

"I suppose a couple of days on the beach . . ." Bolan said agreeably.

"A question, my friends," Beaufort said. "Will you travel together?"

Bolan smiled at Emily. "If you can bring along that white bikini, I think I could put up with your company."

**A different world—
a different war**

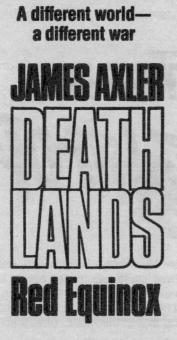

JAMES AXLER

DEATH
LANDS

Red Equinox

Ryan Cawdor and his band of postnuclear survivors enter
a malfunctioning gateway and are transported to Moscow,
where Americans are hated with an almost religious fervor
and blamed for the destruction of the world.

A secret consortium conspires to terrorize the world

DON PENDLETON's
MACK BOLAN
Tightrope

One by one, the top officials of international intelligence agencies are murdered, spearheading a new wave of terrorist atrocities throughout Western Europe. Mack Bolan's mission is compromised from the start. The line between good and evil is a tightrope no man should walk. Unless that man is the Executioner.

Mack Bolan's

PHOENIX FORCE

by Gar Wilson

The battle-hardened, five-man commando unit known as Phoenix Force continues its onslaught against the hard realities of global terrorism in an endless crusade for freedom, justice and the rights of the individual. Schooled in guerrilla warfare, equipped with the latest in lethal weapons, Phoenix Force's adventures have made them a legend in their own time. Phoenix Force is the free world's foreign legion!

"Gar Wilson is excellent! Raw action attacks the reader on every page."

—Don Pendleton

Phoenix Force titles are available wherever paperbacks are sold.

PF-1